WORKING

Romance

Susan Kohler

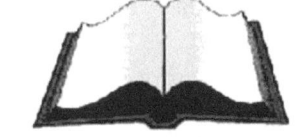

CCB Publishing
British Columbia, Canada

Working Romance

Copyright ©2010 by Susan Kohler
ISBN-13   978-1-926585-95-6
First Edition

Library and Archives Canada Cataloguing in Publication
Kohler, Susan, 1950-
Working romance / written by Susan Kohler – 1st ed.
ISBN 978-1-926585-95-6
Also available in electronic format.
I. Title.
PS3611.O47W67 2010   813'.6   C2010-904654-4

Original cover art design by Jinger Heaston: www.jingraphix.org

Publisher: CCB Publishing
             British Columbia, Canada
             www.ccbpublishing.com

Dedication

To my friend, Laurie Jo, who's always been there for me.
We've had some crazy times, haven't we?

Chapter One

Kate shifted uncomfortably on her beach blanket, very conscious of the tiny grains of sand clinging to her hot skin. To say that she was enjoying her first visit to a local nude beach would be debatable. Her feelings were decidedly mixed. She was a mature, sensuous woman with one exception: she was very shy about her body. Who said a modern woman couldn't be modest?

She did manage to shed all her clothes and lie down on a blanket, but she had not really shed all her inhibitions and relaxed. In spite of the embarrassment, maybe even because of it, Kate was acutely aware of several things that felt different to her about this particular day at the beach.

For one thing, the sun seemed hotter, more intense on her bare skin than it ever had before, and for another, she was more keenly aware of the gritty grains of sand that were scattered on her large, faded blue beach blanket than she had ever been before. Her breasts and buttocks that normally would have been covered with a fairly modest one-piece swimsuit seemed to have developed extremely sensitive nerve endings. Her skin tingled. She was aware of feeling both embarrassed and sensual at the same time, and totally, vibrantly alive. It was a feeling that she had not felt in a very long time.

She was there because her best friend, Laura Kelsey, had talked her into coming. Laura had an outlook on life that was loving, joyous and more than a little reckless. She embraced life fully, with a hint of abandon, whereas Kate held herself back, just a little bit more reserved and quite a bit more wary. That is, Kate was usually fairly cautious except when she was around Laura. Maybe, Kate thought with a silent laugh, this time Laura was right.

Laura would have the nerve to walk into a lion's den naked. She would also probably try to talk Kate into going in with her and usually she was persuasive enough to succeed.

"You'll love it! It feels wonderful, so free and natural. It's hard to explain but I always feel less self-conscious at the nude beach than I do at the regular beach!" Laura had said. Her brown eyes were gleaming as she wiggled her eyebrows, grinned, and added, "Besides the scenery's much better. Come on! It's your last day of freedom before starting the new job and you really need an adventure. Trust me."

"Sure. Yeah. Really." Kate deadpanned, teasing her friend, "Trust me. Now, let me think, where have I heard that before? Hmm, oh I remember, you've conned me with that line ever since we met. 'Trust me' should be your own personal motto. It should be tattooed on your behind."

"Who says it isn't? And you've always loved being conned." Laura reminded her, with a grin, "Especially into some of our more outrageous adventures. It makes it easier to blame me when we both get in trouble."

"Which we always seem to do." Kate smiled at her reckless friend and thought about their friendship.

Laura had been leading Kate into adventures since they met in high school. Their friendship, adventures and pranks both continued unabated right through college and up until they were both married. Their pranks were funny rather than destructive, never causing any damage. When they were caught in a prank, they usually managed to charm their way out of any consequences since the victim was usually laughing.

Now, Laura was the assistant controller at a large electronics corporation in the area. She'd had the job for about six months. In the short time she'd worked there, she had become the right hand and good friend to her new boss. In fact, the more she got to know him, the more she thought he would be perfect for Kate.

Kate had become subdued and withdrawn since she'd been widowed. It was only natural, Laura knew, but she couldn't help thinking that her new boss would be a perfect man to wake Kate up and bring the life back into her eyes. How could he miss? He was single, gorgeous, and had a great personality. Laura had just begun to look for a way to set him up with Kate when an accounting position opened up at the firm.

Luckily, the position became available just as Kate was planning to return to work for the first time since losing her husband. Laura called Kate and told her that Mr. Simmons had left hiring the new clerk in Accounts Payable up to her. The position would be offered on a temp-to-perm basis.

Although there would be a short interview with Mr. Simmons before Kate started to work, she was told to be prepared to stay and begin work after the interview. Laura also hinted about something more, other than Accounts Payable involved in the new job.

Kate realized she was drifting and pulled herself back to the present.

"Tell me again how I'll be less embarrassed with a bare, um, ass than in a bathing suit?" Kate had asked, a bit skeptical about that.

"Because at the regular beach, everybody's looking at you and most of the men are trying to picture how you look naked, right? Well, here there's no pretense. Most of them take a look and leave you alone. There are ways to let them know you want to hang out with them. Of course," she added, with exaggerated self-righteousness, "as a married woman I keep to myself, except for my eyes." The self-righteous tone was ruined by the mischief in her eyes.

Kate laughed as she surrendered to Laura, and quipped, "Okay, I'll go! The idea of naked men to, um, *hang out* with is too good to pass up!"

A part of her really meant it at the time. She conveniently

forgot that whenever she let Laura talk her into an adventure they always got into sticky situations. Besides, how much of an adventure was it to keep your face buried in a book, even if it was the latest thriller by Dean Koontz? So here she was, relaxed, sort of, enjoying the feel of the sun on her back, her buttocks, and her legs, sort of, and trying not to stare at the men too much, well, she admitted to herself with a grin, sort of.

Laura had a book to read, too. She had a new J.D. Robb novel that she read for a while, before she got up and headed for the water. She took a quick dip in the ocean then walked along the beach. Finally she returned to lie on her blanket. After a short nap, she went back for a real swim once again, leaving Kate alone with her nose still in her book.

Kate looked around the small cove, with the high cliffs that kept it private and then looked at the other sunbathers. To her surprise, most of them looked very normal, like any other group of people on any other beach. The ages ranged from young adult to about seventy. They ran the gamut of sizes from quite thin to very large. Among the group were several very good-looking men. Thank goodness.

Although she wasn't man hunting, Kate had to admit to herself ruefully, she appreciated male beauty as much as the next girl. Now that's entertainment, she thought to herself, as she surreptitiously glanced up to watch some well-built young men playing volleyball. The only difference between the others and herself was they all seemed to be totally relaxed and enjoying themselves.

She had to admit to herself that aside from a few lingering glances, no one was paying any special attention to her. In truth, Kate realized, the problem was entirely her own. She began to gradually relax and for Kate, that was a real feat.

Kate was not an old-fashioned woman. She was as self-assured, confident and certainly as passionate as any other woman, and she had a devious sense of humor. She had always been modest except with her husband. With Joe, she had been an aggressive and highly sexual woman, totally confident and comfortable in her own body and fully capable of taking delight in his.

Part of the reason she came with Laura was to see if she could shed her modesty. Eventually, she would have to face the world and begin dating again, although the idea of spending time with any man but Joe left her cold. She couldn't even imagine kissing, let alone having sex with any other man, but deep inside she knew she would. Someday. In the future. If she could ever let a man close to her again. If she ever hoped to have a love life.

She was also curious to see if she could still feel anything sexually. She wanted to find out if any man could even begin to arouse her interest other than a basic admiration of the male body. She was enjoying looking at the men, but so far no one had caused her heart to flutter or pulse to race. Not a bit. Maybe she was just too wound up to enjoy looking, or maybe she hadn't seen the right man yet, she thought, after all looks weren't everything. There was still hope.

She hadn't relaxed enough to turn over and expose her breasts but she would have to soon. If she didn't, she would be too sunburned to sit down when she started her new job. One thing she had forgotten was Laura's passion for lying out in the sun for too long. Too long for Kate at least, because while Laura tanned beautifully, and the sun lightened and streaked her curly, caramel colored hair, Kate turned into a lobster, no matter how much sunscreen she used. Of course, the sun also turned her hair into a dull, brittle mess. Nature, Kate thought wryly, was a very unfair witch.

Just when Kate was working up her nerve to turn over, Laura exclaimed, "Well! I'll be damned! I've never seen *him* here before."

There was a hint of alarm in her voice.

"Who?" Kate was only mildly interested; she didn't even

look up.

"Bob Simmons." Laura hesitated, then started talking too fast, sounding alarmed. "Ah . . . Kate, I'm sorry. This is the first time I ever saw anyone I knew here, and it had to be Bob, of all people."

"So who the heck is Bob?" By now Kate was concerned, she had noticed the consternation in Laura's voice. She knew it took something major to upset Laura.

"Kate, I'm truly sorry about this," Laura couldn't meet Kate's eyes, "As of tomorrow, he's your new boss."

"He's my what?" Kate gave a shriek, only partly muffled by her beach blanket. She thought she was embarrassed before but now she knew what the word really meant.

"Your new boss. The man you're going to work for, starting tomorrow." Laura said, eyes laughing, "Please, please don't kill me!"

Laura was really worried about her best friend's reaction to this latest sticky situation. She watched as Kate buried her face in the towel. How was she going to set these two up if Kate died of terminal embarrassment, she wondered, but then again, the little voice in her mind added, even Kate could hardly ignore Bob now. Heaven's above, she looked up at Bob as he walked over and thought to herself, no woman breathing could ignore him, even a very happily married woman like herself.

"No! Laura, I can't let him see me here. No way I'm going to meet my new boss stark, staring naked! How could I ever face him at work? Is he really headed this way? How do I hide?" There was genuine panic in Kate's voice.

"Too late," Laura whispered, then she looked up and smiled. "Hi Bob! I didn't know you came to this beach."

"I've never been here before. I just moved in up on the bluffs," Bob answered. "Who's your sunburned friend?"

"I'm not sure that's a sunburn, I think she's blushing, and if it's your first time here, why aren't you? Blushing, I mean."

Laura asked, with a hint of challenge in her voice.

"I didn't say I had never been to any nude beach," Bob looked down at the woman trying desperately to disappear into the beach towel, "Just not this one."

He couldn't help but notice three things: She had beautiful, long, red hair, a great ass, and she was so red that she seemed like she was about to die of either sunburn or total embarrassment.

"I noticed you skipped the introduction." He took pity on her. "Hey, don't be shy. Everybody's nervous the first time they're here. Look at it this way, you'll probably never see any of these people again."

He didn't mention that he had every intention of seeing her again, with Laura's help. This brought a muffled choking sound from the blanket and caused Laura to look away.

Bob looked from one woman to the other and had a sudden sinking feeling that was confirmed by Kate's words. "Oh, I'll see you again all right. I'm your new accounting clerk, Kate Winslow, that is, if I still have a chance at the job."

"Kate, come on now, did Laura tell you that I'm such a jerk that I wouldn't hire someone because I saw her at a nude beach? I promise that tomorrow, I'll act like I've never seen you before." He had a soft, yet husky voice that was very intriguing. At any other time, it would have made Kate think of silk sheets.

"Come on Bob. You know I didn't tell her you were a jerk." Laura added, "I did mention a few things like your sexist attitude, your rotten temper and your special rules: No coffee breaks ever. Bow and kiss the floor whenever you walk into the room. Oh, and we have to wash your car on our lunch hour."

"Yeah, but I don't make you wax it," Bob grinned, "not everyday, and if I really were such a sexist pig, her chances for success on the job have just improved a whole lot."

By now Kate had gotten up her nerve to take a quick peek up, just to see if the owner of that intriguing voice looked as good as he sounded. She had, however, failed to realize exactly what part of a naked man kneeling in front of her would be in her immediate field of vision. Her eyes landed on the part of him that would have been covered up at any regular beach.

Oh my, she thought as she gasped, it's been a long time, but if I remember right, that's pretty darn spectacular! Kate knew instantly that her libido was not dead, it was gloriously alive and well. All her dormant hormones began to rage as she also noticed wavy brown hair, bright blue eyes, and a surprisingly muscular build for an accountant. I wonder what he does to get that body into shape, she thought, he didn't build those muscles behind a desk. Her muffled gasp did not go unnoticed by Laura.

"Kate," Bob said, quietly sitting down and discretely laying his light brown towel in his lap, "I can't help noticing that you're embarrassed. Please tell me you're not going to let it stop you from coming in to work tomorrow, are you? You aren't going to chicken out, are you?"

"She certainly will," Laura commented. "She's not only shy but she's also a world champ at second thoughts. If it were an Olympic event, she'd make the team."

Bob considered this for a moment.

"We'll fix it so that she doesn't have time to think. Why don't you two get dressed and come up to the house? I'll fix lunch for you both and we can talk before Kate has a chance to get those second thoughts in gear." Bob offered, "Besides, we have things we can go over before she starts work. You know that I wanted to have a private conference with the two of you outside the office so no one else could overhear. Would barbecued burgers be enough inducement to talk shop for half an hour on your day off? I'll even do all the cooking."

"Can I bring Jack?" Laura asked.

"Sure, why not?" Bob and Jack, Laura's husband, had become good friends.

"So boss man, tell me how to get to your new house and I'll drag Kate along, kicking and screaming." She listened as Bob gave her the directions. "We'll be there in about an hour, okay?"

"Laura, I can't," Kate finally found her voice. "I've got to get the kids from my mom."

"Kate, that's an excuse, she was going to keep them for a couple of hours longer anyway," Laura said firmly. "You might as well give in, because you know I can talk you into anything."

"Why don't you bring them along?" Bob suggested. "Do they like hamburgers?"

"Are you serious? They're kids; they practically live on hamburgers." Meeting his eyes for the first time, Kate continued, "But won't your wife get mad if you invite us over without warning her? And about my kids, I hate to admit it, they can sometimes be little monsters."

"No problem." He gazed into her brilliant green eyes, only peripherally looking at the full swell of her breasts she unconsciously revealed as she raised herself up on her elbows. "I don't have a wife and I firmly believe that all kids are supposed to be little monsters on occasion. At least my mom says I was, and I know I'm practically perfect." He winked, full of humor. "Do you have any other objections?"

At her silence he went on, "Please bring your swimsuits, I've got a pool. Unless you would prefer to go skinny-dipping?" He couldn't resist teasing. "I'll see you in an hour or so."

As he walked away both women were watching, they had to, he had great buns.

Kate and Laura pulled on their clothes. Then they started to gather their things, stuffing their towels, books and sunscreen into Laura's large straw beach bag, and pouring the melted ice out of the small cooler. They opened the last two sodas.

They headed for Laura's car and put all their things in the backseat. Kate was still arguing that she didn't want to go to Bob's house.

"Shut up already! It's for your own good. I know you better than you know yourself, and I know that if you wait until tomorrow you'll worry about it all night. You'll make it into such a major problem in your mind that by morning you'll be a basket case. I don't know why it bothers you so much that Bob saw you naked but I know you well enough to know that it does," Laura explained, feeling like a kidnapper as she pushed a reluctant Kate into her car.

Once she had Kate in the car, Laura quickly flipped through her CD's, choosing Clay Aiken for the drive home.

Kate continued to protest. "I'm just a prude, I guess, the old cliché of a lonely widow who's forgotten all about sex."

"With all those kids, how the heck can you have forgotten about sex? And, you don't really have to be a celibate widow, you know. Even with all the dangers out there, like rotten men and worse diseases, I could still set you up. Jack has a lot of nice friends."

"Sure, Jack has lots of friends that want a widow with three kids, all under six. Besides, if I didn't know better, I'd say that you have already set me up." Kate was suddenly suspicious. "I wonder why you never mentioned that my new boss was such a hunk."

"Bob, a hunk? I never noticed!" Laura exclaimed. "After all, I'm a married woman."

She eyed Kate speculatively. She really hadn't planned for it to happen, but she was glad it had. They would make a great couple and she was an inveterate matchmaker.

"You're not blind, just married and not too married to notice a face like that, and the body? The muscles? Even Jack wouldn't buy that one," Kate threatened. "I'm going to tell Jack to spank you for lying!"

"Jack would love it but I'd rather pass until my butt wasn't sunburned, if you don't mind," Laura said giggling. "Bob *is* very good looking, isn't he? He's also very nice, thoughtful and considerate, well-built, well-off, not at all a sexist pig, amazing as that is these days, and he can be funny as heck. Hell no, I would never set you up with a man like that."

"Of course you would, brat. For once, however, I don't mind half as much as you think I do. Did you notice, uh, his uh, how do I put it?" Kate searched for a tactful word.

"Who wouldn't?" Laura exclaimed, needing no further explanation. "It was rather hard to ignore, wasn't it?" She pulled the car into her driveway and parked. "He had a great backside, too. Hi Honey!"

Her husband looked up from working on his car, a classic red Ford Mustang. A big smile crossed his handsome face, his brown eyes filled with warm humor.

"It's the perverted women! See anyone better than me?" He took one look at Kate's face and added, "Oh, oh! If Kate's face is anything to go by, it looks like maybe you did. I think I'm jealous." He grinned, absently rubbing one hand on what might once have been a white T-shirt.

"Dear, you know you're the only man on earth for me. I can't imagine who Kate saw. I didn't see anybody special, because I wasn't looking. I couldn't care less about other men," Laura replied, but her cheeks were a little flushed. She kissed him. "After all, I've already got the best."

"Stand in the garden while you talk like that, Dearie, it needs the fertilizer," Jack replied, turning her towards the garden with his hands on her shoulders and patting her behind. "I know you look at other men, just like I know that you'll always come home to me. So, who was he?"

She turned back to face him and gave up all pretense. "We ran into Bob Simmons. He invited us to lunch and if you're nice you can come along." She turned to Kate, "Go, call your mom, and then take a shower. I'll go over and get the kids and something for you to wear, while you're getting ready. Jack, don't let her leave. I just know she's going to turn chicken!"

"Why can't I go get my kids and meet you there?" Kate was looking for a way out. "And why can't I wear these?"

11

"Because I know you, you'll try to escape," Laura said, "and because I can think of about a dozen things you have that look better on you, so stop arguing and get going. Go!"

"Okay, you wicked witch, I'll be good." But there was a hint of the devil in Kate's eyes.

"Why would Kate be so upset just because you ran into Bob at the beach?" Jack asked, then realized the answer. "Oh, forget I asked, *Miss Modesty*. Man, I wish I'd been there. I can see it all now. Wow Kate! What a place for you to get the first glimpse of your new boss." He said with a laugh, "My wife strikes again. Okay. Laura, you go get the kids. I'll keep Kate from escaping. Kate, call your mom, then start getting ready. I'll finish this car and put my tools away. Don't use up all the hot water." Jack ducked back under the hood.

"Masterful, ain't he?" Laura remarked, rolling her eyes as the two women went into the house.

"Laura, I should go get the kids myself, then I can shower and change at home," Kate pleaded, giving it one more try.

"No way!" Laura protested, "I'm not letting you out of my sight without Jack guarding you. No joke, you really would chicken out."

The two women stopped in Laura's kitchen while Kate called her mother. She told her mom that Laura was driving over to pick up the kids. Before she had a chance to hang up, Laura grabbed the phone away from her.

"Hold on a second, Betty." She covered the receiver and turned to Laura. "Hit the shower."

"Okay, I give up." Kate grinned. "You'll pester me to death if I don't."

She went upstairs to Laura's bedroom, wondering what mischief Laura and her mom would get into over the phone.

Kate wound up taking an extra long shower because her mind kept wandering. As she soaped her body, she kept picturing Bob. His body and his smile were replayed in her mind. At one point in the shower, she could almost feel his hands running over her body, sensually soaping her. She pulled herself back to reality. Kate was surprised at how erotic her thoughts had been while she washed herself. Maybe Laura was right; maybe she had been alone too long. Maybe it was time for her to begin looking forward.

When Kate got out of the shower, she sat on the edge of Laura's king-sized bed wrapped in a towel and dried her hair. With one corner of her mind, she noticed that the usually neat Laura had left her bed unmade. By the time her hair was dry, she heard the familiar voices outside; Laura had already returned with the kids and a sundress for Kate to wear.

Laura came into the bedroom with a dress on a hanger and a small bag in her hands. She pulled Kate into the bathroom and handed her the bag, which contained her cosmetics, and a pair of lacy panties. No bra, Kate noted, and wondered what dress her mom had sent. Laura sat on the edge of the bathtub while Kate put on her make-up and fixed her hair.

She told Kate, "The little darlings are outside with Jack. We were lucky, your mom had just cleaned them up and they actually look almost angelic."

"False advertising." There was pride in her voice in spite of the words as Kate pulled the dress off the hanger. "Hey, brat. Since when did you get too lazy to make your bed?"

Laura grinned. "I did make up my bed this morning, but somehow it got unmade again."

"Ah, the infamous five-year-long honeymoon. May it never end." Kate smiled back, then leaned closer to the mirror to finish her face.

She couldn't help noticing that Laura had picked out her sexiest sundress. It was a low cut halter-top that left her back bare, it had big, bright yellow and orange flowers. Thanks to Kate's skill with needle and thread, there was a lace insert for the neckline that served to cover most of her cleavage. Before bringing the dress over, Laura had thoughtfully removed the insert.

"I see you managed to sabotage my dress." She looked at Laura with mild accusation. "Where's the rest of the neckline?"

"Don't thank me now, wait until later." Laura grinned unabashed. "Besides I didn't know that the lace would come off, you'll have to thank your mother for telling me that. I'm going to take a shower."

"I'd better go rescue Jack from my little angels." Kate went in search of her kids. When she found them, they were outside helping Jack put away his tools.

"Hey Jack, do you need to be rescued from these rug rats?" Kate gave all three of her kids a big warm group hug. "You look like you have all the help you can use."

His newfound help consisted of twin three-year-old girls, and a boy of five.

"Don't tell Laura I told you, but I could use help like this all the time." He good-naturedly retrieved a screwdriver from little fingers, and smiled down at the tiny hand tugging on the leg of his faded jeans.

He looked up and grinned at Kate with pride and excitement in his eyes. "And it looks like I'm going to get it fairly soon."

"Why hasn't Laura told me?" She grabbed Jack and kissed him. "That's wonderful!"

He grinned. "It sure is. I think Laura meant to tell you about it today but you two seem to have been distracted. I wonder why." He gently wiped little fingers. "It couldn't have anything to do with meeting Bob, could it? While you both were N A K E D?" Jack spelled, teasing her gently. "Here, you can have the terrible trio back while I go get cleaned up."

Chapter Two

It was still early afternoon when they all landed on the doorstep of Bob's large, two-story house. The six of them, three adults and three small children made a boisterous and colorful group. Laura and Kate were both in sundresses; Laura's was a hot pink that looked great against her dark blond hair. Kate's bright yellow print set off her curvy figure. Jack was in light blue shorts and a brightly colored Hawaiian shirt.

"Hi! Come on in. Who are these little people?" Bob greeted the group, smiling at the three children. He looked cool and wonderful in navy shorts and a white polo shirt.

Kate was proud as she introduced the kids. She smiled down at the girls. "The twins are Suzy and Sarah, and they're not nearly as angelic as they look," she warned. "But I think I'll keep 'em anyway."

"Mom, you said we were your little angels," Suzy protested.

"You are sweetie, but only to me," Kate told her, hugging the small girl.

The little girls did indeed look like little angels dressed in frilly pink dresses. They had big green eyes and golden blond curls.

"And this guy is Sam, who certainly is no angel; he's all boy." Kate ruffled his hair, getting a scowl for her efforts.

Sam had brown eyes, freckles, and his hair was dark red. He had a defiant expression on his little face. He wore red shorts and a Ninja Turtle T-shirt.

"I can see where Sam got his hair, but the girls got your eyes, didn't they?" Bob bent down to the kids. "Hi guys. I'm glad you came over with your mom."

"This is Mr. Simmons." Kate introduced Bob.

The little girls both greeted Bob with nervous giggles, clinging to Kate's skirt.

Sam looked up at Kate and demanded loudly, "Mommy, I want to go home!"

"Gee, Sam, I guess you don't want to have some hamburgers and go swimming," Kate said quietly. "You must be feeling sick; maybe I'd better take you to the doctor."

"I'm okay, Mommy. We can stay," Sam said quickly.

"Let's go out on the patio, I've got the charcoal started." Bob ignored Sam's outburst as he looked down at the three small visitors.

"Would you like some hamburgers?" Bob asked. The kids all nodded, even Sam. Turning to the adults he added, "I fixed a salad and set up the barbecue. Does that sound okay?"

At their nods, he went on, "I have beer, sodas, milk, orange juice, and iced tea in the refrigerator, everyone serve yourself."

Soon they were all sitting at the patio table with iced tea. The kids ran around the yard, slowing down only long enough to take sips of orange juice. Bob started grilling hamburgers, and everyone fixed their own buns, except for the kids. They also had the salad, fries, and corn on the cob.

By the time they started to eat, Kate found her initial self-consciousness fading and she began to enjoy herself. Surprisingly enough, the afternoon was really turning out to be fun! Kate thanked the heavens that for once her brood seemed to be willing to eat without pulling any of their customary mealtime squabbles, except for a minor food fight with some French fries. She quickly quelled the spat.

"Kate, why did you say your kids are not the little angels they appear to be? So far they seem very well behaved," Bob asked her curiously.

"Well, they have been pretty good today. As a matter of fact, they really are pretty good kids." She paused, smiling proudly at her brood, "But I always warn people because that way if the kids are fairly good it makes them seem even better, but if they're cranky or bad, people shrug it off and figure that they were warned."

"In other words, either way, people figure that the kids aren't as bad as you thought they'd be." Bob poured her more iced tea. "Very sneaky!"

"For 'people' you can read in her mother-in-law, who thinks all children should be quiet, polite, and neat practically from the moment of birth," Laura said. "These three are plenty old to be taught some manners, in her words."

"She meant every word when she said that, Laura, but remember, that was when she was almost beside herself with grief and loss. She's more like her old self lately. In fact, she's mellowed quite a lot, now that she has more friends with their own grandchildren who really do make my three look like little angels. It's just that after we lost Joe, she went through a period where she was bitter and felt all alone. She really wasn't herself. Her husband had died, less than three months before she lost her son. Joe was her only child." Kate paused, remembering how broken Ida had been. "She shielded herself by turning very cold and controlling. She decided to take over raising my children to fill the void in her life, but she's a totally different person now."

"Is she really?" Laura asked. "What caused the change?"

"I forgot, I haven't told you yet. She has a hot new man in her life. His name is George. He takes her dancing, bowling, and out to play golf. He has definitely loosened her up *and* he has three small grand-kids that really make my kids all look like monks, not monkeys." Kate smiled, "He's so good for her. He's even good with my kids."

"That's great!" Laura said, remembering the woman she had met long ago. "Before everything happened, she always used to be such a free-spirited woman. She was so colorful and bursting with life and energy. I could never understand how she could turn out to be so formal and cold with your kids. It was like

Jekyll and Hyde."

"It took George to help me understand." Kate smiled sadly, "It was fear. Fear of losing someone else, fear of being hurt again, that's what made her so aloof. It helped her keep her distance, emotionally."

Just then the kids started to beg Bob to go swimming in the pool. Kate tried without very much success to remind them that they should wait to be invited.

"But what if he never invites us to swim?" Sam, ever argumentative with his little lower lip sticking out a mile added, "Then we won't ever get to go swimming. We never get to have any fun."

"It's hard to argue with that kind of thinking," Bob told the boy, smiling, "but I suspect your mom's right and you should wait until I ask you if you want to swim. Guess I was being awfully slow to ask, wasn't I?" He looked over at Kate. "Can they swim?"

"Like little fishes, but I watch them like a hawk, if that isn't a mixed metaphor," Kate replied. "Anyway, it's too soon after lunch."

"So just go slowly putting all of them into their swimsuits," Laura suggested, "or try to get them to take a short nap first."

"Nap? Nap? It's obvious you don't have kids. Naps are for moms, not for kids. You can go tell the mini-monsters that they have to take a nap before they can swim," Kate challenged her. "I'll just stay here and wait to pick up the pieces after they tear you apart."

"Wouldn't it be better if we could get them to watch some videos? That would give us a chance to talk business before we swim," Bob suggested. Noting the women's startled expressions, he added, "I have six nieces and four nephews."

Kate never quite knew what happened next but a short time later the gruesome threesome was lying on the floor in Bob's den with Jack, watching THE LITTLE MERMAID. All the doors to the outside were locked, plus the gate between the house and the pool. Even so, Jack had been admonished that one of the little dears might wake up and decide to go swimming without waiting for the adults.

"Watch the children, not the movie, and stay awake, okay?" Laura told her husband. "We're going to talk business."

"Nag, nag, nag," Jack muttered, his eyes fixed on the television.

Bob, Laura, and Kate picked up the remains from lunch and took things into the kitchen. Working as a team, they cleaned up the few dishes from lunch. When they had put the leftovers into the refrigerator, they sat at the small kitchen table.

Laura opened the conversation. "Bob, I didn't fill Kate in on all the details about the special problems that we're having at work, so maybe we'd better do that, now."

"What's up?" Kate asked. "Is it the job?"

"In a way," Bob replied, pouring them all some more iced tea. "You see, we've been having trouble with employee theft at work. Not just petty theft, but embezzlement. Every time we hire a new clerk in the accounting department, we start losing money. The evidence always seems to point to the new clerk. Someone wanted it to look like we were hiring dishonest people but we're not that dumb. Four times now, when we've got a new employee, money starts disappearing. We know someone is hiding his own larceny by hiding behind the new hires. The thefts stop when the latest employee leaves, until I replace them, then they soon start occurring again. That's why we wanted to hire someone one of us knew personally. It's also why your past auditing experience is so important. The gist of it is: we want you to help us to catch the thief. Of course, the rest of the staff will think we just got you from the temp agency, like we usually do."

"So I'll be undercover, like on TV, but who else is in on it?" Kate asked. "And is there really a permanent job after I catch the bad guy?"

"No one knows but Bob and myself, and of course, one person at corporate headquarters," Laura answered. "And yes, there is a real job after you find the thief. I think it'll be in auditing and cost accounting, not the accounts payable department. Once we find out who we have to replace and decide how we need to restructure accounting, we will bring in some new people. By the way, we also helped the other employees who fell under suspicion find new jobs. Except for one girl who went on pregnancy leave, and she does some work for us online from home."

"She's such a good worker we couldn't let her go," Bob added. "The other three employees weren't officially fired by the way; we just told the office staff that their jobs were being phased out due to cutbacks. Then we got them placed in new jobs we helped find for them. Shelly's baby is due in about five weeks so she won't be back until we get this problem resolved. By the way Kate, do you have a computer at home?"

"No," she told him. "I was thinking about getting one. Should I?"

"Don't bother. I'll loan you one from the office and set you up so that you can work online. Just let me know if you ever need to stay home and you can work from there. It will benefit both of us. I've never met a working mother who didn't have problems once in a while with a sick kid or the sitter. Also, you might want to work on some of your investigating at home so I'll be sure to get it to you and arrange to pay any charges."

Laura took over. "The plan is that tomorrow you show up at eight, and we claim that you're just a temp we got from the employment agency. Of course, you and I don't know each other, but I always get to know the new people first. Last of all, depending on how it goes, at some point you might need to be treated as a suspect. That may probably be when you need to do some investigating at home. We'll call attention to your poor attendance and constant tardiness and use that as an excuse to suspect you. It'll all be an act so go along with it," Laura said. "Of course, you'll be well compensated for any work you do at home. Is that it, Bob? Is it time for us to swim?"

"Now Laura, wait until you've been asked," Kate said, primly, reminding them of the children waiting to swim. They all laughed.

"I'll show you where you can change into your suits," Bob laughed, standing up. He led them into a large bathroom downstairs. "There's already plenty of towels out by the pool."

Laura and Kate both changed into their swim suits. Laura had a red polka dot bikini. Kate expected to find her modest black one-piece in the bag her mom had sent over with Laura, but instead she found an emerald green bikini. It was a suit Laura had talked her into buying but that Kate had seldom worn. She put it on, deciding it wasn't so bad after all, at least the color brought out the color of her eyes.

"I'm going to go rescue Jack and unleash the monsters," she told Laura. "Wait here and you can help me get them into their suits, then the last one in is a rotten egg!"

All seven of them had quite a ball in the pool, even if the four adults had to keep a close watch on the three little ones. Bob had plenty of floats and inflatable toys for the kids to play with. Soon they had a great game of "try to sink Jack" going that was highlighted by Kate grabbing for Jack and getting her hands on Bob's trunks by mistake.

Startled green eyes met shocked blue eyes in a look that almost caused the water to boil. Both of them were very conscious of the other, and of Kate's hands, and just where they accidentally came into contact with Bob's body. It was a long moment, charged with a current of electricity that didn't escape the notice of Laura and Jack. With the unspoken, almost psychic, communication that some married couples share, Laura and Jack decided to do a little more matchmaking. Before they could do anything about it, however, Kate's energy gave out and she started to hint that it was time to gather up the kids and go home. Laura gave Jack a sharp kick and he quickly decided to save his shins by stepping in.

"Hey Kate, why don't you just relax for a while in the last of the sun and I'll . . ." He thought fast then blurted out, "I'll take the kids out for some ice cream?"

Her eyes narrowed. "Dammit Jack, you know better than to ask me a question like that when the little dears can hear you! Now I have to be the bad guy and say no."

"No, you don't," Jack pleaded. "Just say yes. You know I'll take good care of them. Please, it's the only way Laura will let me break my diet."

He gave her a pathetic, hound-dog look, innocence shining in his warm brown eyes.

"What diet? You're in great shape."

"How do you think I keep in shape?" Jack begged. "Kate let me take them, please?"

Kate relented, laughing, "Okay, take them away, I'm going to lay on that chaise lounge and relax."

It seemed like it had been an extra long day to Kate, full of tension and emotional ups and downs. She was tired, drained by the late summer sun, and felt so curiously restless that she hardly noticed when the kids finally left with Jack. She was not even consciously aware that Laura had gone with them. She had almost drifted off to sleep when suddenly a fresh glass of iced tea appeared in front of her face.

"Alone at last," Bob quipped softly, raising his eyebrows suggestively. "I thought they'd never leave. You do know our mutual friends are playing matchmaker, don't you?"

"Don't let it worry you, I plan to murder them soon," she threatened, eyes narrowed. "Real soon."

"That's funny. I was thinking of giving Laura a big raise," Bob replied.

He took a long swallow of his iced tea before he said, "I

brought out some sun block, roll over and I'll put it on you."

"I can do it myself." She regarded him a little warily.

They were both ignoring the fact that it was too late in the afternoon for the sun to be a big problem, and of course, that Kate was lying on her back.

"Trust me." He grinned, and waited while she rolled over.

"You really have been working with Laura too long, that's her line. It's what she used to get me to the beach today." She flushed a little at the memory. "Yikes! That's cold!" She yelled as he poured the sunscreen onto her silky skin.

Soon she relaxed and gave herself over to the stroking of his large but gentle hands. She almost pouted when he finished putting the lotion on her.

"Bob?" she asked, raising up on one arm and turning to look over her shoulder at him, "Did she set me up today?"

"No. Kate, I swear I had no idea the two of you were going to be there." There was pleasure and just a hint of guilt is his grin. "I won't swear that I'm sorry you were there. To put it right out in the open, I liked what I saw."

"What you saw, ha! You should have seen my view." She rolled onto her back and slanted him a mischievous glance. "Bigger than a breadbox."

Bob almost choked on his iced tea. "Here I thought you were so shy! I'm shocked!" He actually blushed.

"I don't know what you're talking about. You're at least six-foot tall, certainly bigger than a breadbox. Unless you thought I meant, ah, a little over-confident, are we?" She laughed openly at his expression.

"You led me into that!" he accused. "You are a minx under those blushes." He eyed her for a long moment silently, speculating. "Do you think kisses constitute sexual harassment?"

"I think that depends on who's kissing who, and how, and why, and what kind of kisses." She grinned, and raised her eyebrows. "You'll have to give me a little more to go on if you want a definitive answer," she challenged.

He reached a hand out and slid it behind her neck, pulling her gently towards him. "Is this definitive enough?"

It was no ordinary first kiss. There was no tentative, gentle exploration. He kissed her with a passion that left them both breathless, boldly sliding his tongue into her mouth. I'm in trouble, she thought, wonderful trouble. She met his passion with her own, putting as much into the kiss as he did.

Finally, breathing heavily, she managed to reply to his question. "Whew! I know for sure that would constitute sexual harassment to anyone at the office."

"But not to you?" He cocked his head to one side inquisitively.

She laid back on the chaise lounge, acting nonchalant and said innocently, "How could it? I've never even been to the office."

"Why did I get the idea that you were so timid and shy?" He looked at her quizzically.

"You've been underestimating me just because I blush, sir!" She sat up again and began to lean towards him. "You should have known better. After all, I have three small kids and a best friend like Laura. How naive could I be?"

She stopped talking as her mouth almost reached his. Her eyes were as big as saucers as she brought up one hand and traced the outline of his mouth with a slender finger. She slid the hand around his neck and gently touched her mouth to his in a gentle kiss.

"This is probably a bad idea, dangerous, unprofessional and all that jazz, do you care?" she whispered against his warm mouth.

"Not a bit." He kissed her back, pushing her back down on the chaise lounge and laying slightly on top of her.

It was an electric kiss, full of fire and passion. He worked his tongue gently around inside her mouth. They broke apart, both breathing heavily, and looking slightly dazed.

"We may both be in trouble here," Bob said.

"I laugh at trouble, mister!" she intoned dramatically.

"Just so you don't laugh at me." Bob claimed her mouth yet again.

"Who's laughing?" she whispered breathlessly. "Besides how much trouble can we be in if the kids are coming back soon?"

"Want to know a secret? I have plenty of ice cream in the freezer." Bob nibbled her ear. "I just failed to mention it to Jack because I wanted to get rid of everyone."

"Somehow I knew that. Good uncles with children's video libraries and swimming pools surrounded by floating toys always have plenty of ice cream in the freezer, at least during the summer. I think it's a state law." Kate gave herself completely over to the sensations that threatened to overwhelm her, stroking his hair and meeting the thrust of his tongue with her own in a passionate kiss.

Slowly he left her mouth and trailed kisses down her throat, as he slid his hand inside her swimsuit and cupped her breast teasing her nipple with his thumb and forefinger. She moaned with delight.

"Am I moving too fast?" Bob asked softly. "I don't usually come on so-"

"Yes," she interrupted him gently, "but so am I, and I don't act like this with every man I meet either."

"I know that," Bob assured her.

They both tried to ease up but it had been a very long time since Kate had let herself be close to a man, and with Bob everything felt so right and natural that she entirely forgot herself. She forgot all about the three little kids returning soon. She forgot that this was a man that she'd met just today. She even forgot that this man was her new boss, starting tomorrow. And she made him forget, too.

She just felt alive, totally alive in every cell of her being. She also felt his hands on the strings holding the top of her bathing suit . . . they heard a car door slam loudly. The sound was followed quickly by her children's laughter. Instantly his hands dropped away and she adjusted her suit. She tried to look as though nothing was happening.

"I don't know if that was lousy timing or good timing, but I wish they hadn't returned just yet," Bob muttered as he stood up.

"I wish they hadn't come back now either," Kate met his gaze squarely, before admitting softly, "but it's probably a good thing they did."

"Explosive, wasn't it?" Bob kissed her once and walked away.

By the time the others came out to the patio Bob was sitting at the picnic table, with a towel draped over his lap, sipping iced tea and Kate was lying on the chaise lounge pretending to be asleep. Laura and Jack might even have been fooled, if it wasn't for the silly smile on Kate's face.

Laura woke her up. "Having a good dream?"

"What?" She tried to act drowsy and puzzled.

"No one smiles like that when they're just sleeping," Laura said sternly.

"Maybe it's just been a good day." Kate tried to hide her smile but it broke through. "So what?"

"So if that's all it is, Jack dragged us all out for ice cream for nothing. But I'd bet my last nickel that things got pretty hot while we were gone." Laura gave her friend a mischievous smirk. "I have a secret for you, if you'll tell me yours."

"Not here, I wouldn't want Bob to think I'm the kind to kiss and tell. What's yours?" Kate tried not to let Laura know that she already knew, but she failed. "I know, I'll bet you're finally pregnant, aren't you?"

"Witch!" Laura grinned widely, pretending to cuff Kate on the shoulder. "You were supposed to let me tell you."

"What does Jack think?" She certainly didn't want to let Laura know that Jack had already told her.

"He's so excited that he's floating on clouds, he loves kids." She smiled. "Look at him with yours."

"Does Bob know?" Kate asked. "Or anyone else at the office?"

"No, not yet," Laura smiled. "But Bob will be happy for me; he's been nagging me to start a family."

A small cranky voice broke in. "Mommy, can we go home now?" Suzy was getting tired and bored since all the real fun seemed to be over.

"That's my cue, I'd better round up the brat pack." Kate stood up and called the kids. "Okay guys, pick up all your things, we're going to go home."

She walked over to Bob. "Thanks for lunch and letting the kids go swimming. We had fun." She smiled at him.

"I sure hope you did." He winked at her, "I did."

He glanced around and said with a soft voice, "Somehow, I can't say good-bye to you quite the way I'd like to with all these little people here. Or even those two big people." Bob smiled into her eyes. "You will show up in the morning, won't you? You won't have any second thoughts?"

"I'll definitely have second thoughts but I can guarantee you that they won't keep me from showing up at work tomorrow. Nothing could do that now," she said softly

"Good. I'll see you in the morning; it was really spectacular meeting you. Goodnight." He squeezed her hand softly.

Kate returned the gentle squeeze, not trusting herself to speak. Bob nodded, and then he went over to say good-bye to the kids. Kate walked over to Jack.

"Hey, I get to repeat my congratulations, Daddy." She hugged him. "I don't think Laura knows you let the cat out of the bag."

She looked at her kids and grinned. "By the way, thanks for taking my kids out for ice cream, even if you did try to apply it to them externally. Next time, you might try to get some of it *in*

27

their mouths."

All three of the kids had ice cream smeared all over their swimsuits, hands and faces.

"No problem, Kate. Except for the part about getting the ice cream into their little mouths." Jack looked her over speculatively. "Are you interested in him?"

He nodded his head towards Bob.

"Well, he's about a thousand percent better than the last guy Laura tried to get me together with, but I'm going to be working for him. You know how tricky situations like that can be." She surprised even herself by answering him seriously.

Jack gave her a quick grin. "Well, after knowing my wife all these years, you should be an Olympic champ at handling tricky situations."

"So true, but I'm only the silver medalist," she laughed, hugging him. "Laura's got the gold, in more ways than one."

She began to load her kids into the car seats, strapping and buckling everyone in. When Kate finished getting all the kids fastened in, she turned around.

"Hey Jack?" she said with a grin.

"What?" He seemed distracted.

"You and Laura rode with me, remember?" she prodded.

"In other words, I'd better go fetch my wife." He turned to go but Laura came up behind him.

"Are we leaving?" She looked in the minivan. "Dumb question, the kids are all strapped in."

She pinched Jack on his behind. "So get in, Buns."

Just as Jack climbed into the minivan Suzy asked, "Mommy, why did Aunt Laura call Uncle Jack Buns?"

Just as Kate was trying to figure out a good answer for that one, Sarah answered, "Dummy! It's because Uncle Jack ate so many hamburgers!"

The sound of adult laughter filled the minivan.

Chapter Three

The next morning was Kate's first day of work in over five years, since shortly before Sam had been born. She was at various times: anxious, excited, and filled with nervous energy and secret anticipation at the prospect of seeing Bob again.

With all that going on, of course it turned out to be one of *those* mornings. The kind of morning working moms are all too familiar with. She had quite a struggle getting the kids out of bed, not to mention dressed and fed, before dropping them off at her parents' house, and getting herself to the office.

First, the twins had a food fight with the cereal and she had to change their clothes. There was spilled milk, sugar, and corn flakes all over the kitchen table, and dirty dishes in the sink. Then she started to put the kids into the van but she couldn't find Sam. When last seen, he had gone outside to play with the dogs so Kate went into the backyard to look for him.

When she found Sam, he was crawling under a hedge trying to retrieve a missing dog toy. He was muddy, dirty, and his T-shirt, his *new* T-shirt, was torn. She was running too late to bother trying to change him into clean clothes. Just to be on the safe side, she grabbed clean shorts and T-shirts for all three kids, gathered her brood and got them into her slightly battered van.

The kids were firmly strapped into their car seats but still cranky from being dragged out of the house at such an early hour, so the ride to her parents' house was anything but peaceful and quiet. She was glad when she finally got there and deposited the little angels with her mother. She handed the spare clothes over to her mom with a sigh of gratitude.

"Thanks Mom, I'll pick them up after work. Be sure to tell

Dad I said that I love him." She grinned ruefully. "I realized one thing this morning."

"What's that, dear?" Her mother's eyes sparkled with humor as she took in the bedraggled kids; Sam still dressed in his dirty shorts and the torn t-shirt, and noticed Kate's air of nervous frustration.

"I should have listened more closely to your lectures on birth control." She said it absolutely deadpanned, and it took a moment for it to sink in.

"What a terrible thing to say about these little darlings!" Her mother laughed knowingly as she let the kids into the house. "But it does give me a small sense of justice to see them running you ragged. You were quite a handful."

"Oh please, give me strength. I was nothing compared to Sam." Kate rolled her eyes. "And that's not even mentioning the twins. You had it easy. I'd better run or I'll be late for my first day."

Somehow, Kate made it to the office on time. She arrived at the large, glass-covered office building at five minutes to eight looking cool, poised, and professional in a navy pinstripe suit with an ivory silk blouse. Although she had been told that the office had a business casual dress code, for her first day she had decided to wear her most professional and businesslike suit. She wanted to try to erase all traces of her appearance from the day before out of Bob's memory.

The truth was, however, that deep down she hoped it took a lot more than a dignified business suit to make Bob forget his first sight of her. The only hint of the fire in her nature was a hot pink bow that somehow managed not to clash with her deep red hair.

She walked up to a slender, young black woman who was drinking coffee at the receptionist's desk.

"Hello, I'm Kate Winslow, I'm a temporary who's starting work here today, and I'm supposed to ask for Mr. Simmons," she said, smiling at the woman. "Could you please direct me to him?"

"Hi! Welcome to the madhouse. I'm Cheryl, the receptionist at this zoo. I'll take you in to Mr. Simmons' office. Please, follow me." She led Kate to a corner office and knocked on the door. "Bob, the new temp from the agency is here."

"Come in, I'm Bob Simmons. Welcome to Lassen-McRoe." Bob looked wonderful in charcoal gray pants and a crisp, pale blue shirt. His tasteful, conservative clothes, however, were topped off by a wildly colorful tie. He shook her hand and then gestured at a chair and said, "Please, have a seat. Would you like some coffee?"

Cheryl, who was still standing at the door, volunteered to go get her some coffee and a donut. As soon as she had gone, Bob looked at Kate and gave her a wink that sent a chill clear down her spine.

"I hope you really appreciate how cool and professional I'm being today," he said with a grin.

"I do, at least I guess I do," Kate admitted, looking around. "But I have to confess, I hope it isn't too easy. Nice, *very* nice, but is this a business office or one of those snooty British men's clubs?"

Bob had a very large, formal office, with dark wood paneled walls. There were several framed oil paintings depicting fox hunting scenes hanging on the walls and a deep red plaid carpet on the floor. He had a dark red genuine leather armchair and a matching sofa. A triangular table in the corner had a brass lamp on it. Bob's desk was mahogany, and huge. He also had a brass floor lamp. There was a large potted fern in the corner, and to top it all off there was a wood and brass ceiling fan.

"It is kind of anachronistic, isn't it? It used to be the office of the Chairman of the Board until corporate was moved back to Texas. His wife thought she was a decorator. I inherited it. I'll admit that I do like it, but I'm glad it's not a men's club where no women are ever allowed. If I had my way, I'd chase you around this big desk, and when I caught you," he grinned, "I'd throw you down on the sofa."

"You couldn't chase me around the desk." Kate flashed him a smile with a bit of the devil in it. "I wouldn't run."

"Vixen!" Bob laughed. "I can tell I'm going to have one heck of a hard time concentrating on my work today."

"Good, that makes two of us." Kate stopped talking abruptly as Cheryl brought in the coffee and some fresh buttermilk donuts, glazed of course.

"Let me finish explaining your job, then I'll introduce you to Laura, my assistant controller. She will show you around the office," Bob was saying calmly, just as Cheryl entered.

They sat there and enjoyed their morning coffee and each other's company for a short time. For all their banter, when they finally got down to business, the sexual electricity sizzling between them turned out not to be a problem. Because they were both mature adults, their personal feelings didn't interfere with their work. It was as if they had both tucked their awareness of each other away somewhere for future reference.

Bob went over the department structure with her, then showed her basics of the computer system, and assigned her a password. Lastly, he went over the last completed ledgers for accounts payable with her. He had been reviewing them at his desk.

Bob then took Kate to Laura's office. It was a decided step down from his both in size and in lavish decoration, however it was more comfortable and tasteful. Laura had the same slate blue carpet as the rest of the office, but her walls were a pale rose instead of the eggshell paint that covered the rest of the offices. She had several framed pastel prints on her walls, and sleek pecan office furniture. The cool professional effect was only slightly spoiled by the stack of papers strewn all over her desk. Laura took Kate around to the workstations, most of them being small cubicles with a computer, a desk, file cabinets and several shelves.

All of them had various decorations and personal touches to provide clues to the personality of their occupants. Laura introduced Kate to everyone in the small accounting department.

Aside from Laura and Cheryl there were four, all women: Rita who did the payroll was an in her mid-fifties, plump and friendly. She had a warm motherly manner. Rita was wearing navy polyester stretch pants and a long flowing white blouse. Her cubicle was filled with potted plants and pictures of children. She told Kate they were all her grandchildren.

Mary and Jennifer, who shared an extra-large cubicle, did the billing. Mary was small, a Latino spitfire in tight blue jeans with long black hair. Jennifer was a young, pretty blond in a short red dress. Their cubicle had several pictures of Mary's little girl and one of Jennifer's boyfriend, and a Firefighting Hunks calendar.

Diana, tall and shapely with short brown hair and an engaging smile, did the bank reconciliations and would work with Kate on accounts payable until it was caught up. She looked neat and professional in a blue print dress. Her cubicle had several hand-drawn cartoons and pictures of her horse on the walls.

There were two other women who worked in the vault room down the hall, Sherry and Tonya. They handled the cash receipts from the eight retail stores in the district. Laura knocked at their door and identified herself, and one of them opened the door from the inside and let her in. She introduced Kate to them. Their office was stark, with only a framed picture of Tonya's kids for decoration, but they had a stereo that was turned up loud, on a classic rock station.

Finally, Kate was shown to her cubicle. It would have been extra large, but she had one whole wall taken up with filing cabinets. Aside from a computer and a calculator, she had a long flexible sorter on her desk. It was filled to the bursting point with alphabetized invoices. There was also a bin on her desk overflowing with already filed purchase orders, packing slips and any other correspondence related to an invoice, also in alphabetical order.

Kate settled in and spent a fairly quiet morning matching the invoices to the packing slips and correspondence, then inputting the information from the ones that formed completed sets into her computer. While she worked, she was also keeping her eyes and ears open.

All she learned that first day was that her co-workers seemed to be good hard workers who enjoyed their jobs. Everyone seemed congenial; no one seemed to be hiding anything. They were all very helpful and pleasant to her. Shortly before noon Laura came over to ask her out to lunch.

"Won't the, um, suspects think it's strange? I mean supposedly we just met and you're my supervisor," Kate reminded her. "After all I'm supposed to be undercover."

"No, it shouldn't seem suspicious. I almost always take the new girls out to lunch," Laura explained. "Just to welcome them to the company."

"Even the temps?" Kate asked skeptically.

"Well, not the temps, but I don't think it'll give us away," Laura replied. "Besides, I'm the boss, what can they say?"

"In that case, great. I'd love lunch." The pair left quickly.

Kate almost had to run to keep up with Laura as she hurried over to her car. "Hey! What's the rush?" she complained, as she stumbled in the high heels she hadn't worn in almost five years.

"I'm trying to avoid any tag-a-longs, so we can talk." They got into Laura's car and she practically peeled out of the parking lot before continuing, "You are doing some investigating for us, remember?"

"James Bond never had to run to lunch," Kate pointed out, still panting a little.

"James Bond was only trying to catch Russian spies, not avoid office gossips," Laura laughed, "and spies are a lot easier to fool."

"So? Are you buying?" Kate added, "After that fiasco on the beach yesterday morning, you owe me."

"By my account, after taking the kids out for ice cream yesterday afternoon, you owe me lunch. I must be one helluva great matchmaker." Laura looked over at her friend and noted her quick flush. "Aren't I?"

"So what? You think I owe you lunch just because you introduce me to a nice man? I mean, sure, he's very nice, and great looking, and single, has a good job, and kis. . ." Kate stopped quickly, blushing. "What I'm saying is, he's not too bad."

"So he *did* kiss you?" Laura was surprised. "Yesterday? I knew it! That's fantastic! I thought so, I hoped so, but I wasn't sure."

"What's so fantastic?" Kate was suspicious. "We were having a good time together and he kissed me. It was a great kiss, but what's got you so excited? Men and women kiss all the time, you know. They've been doing it for centuries."

"But not you, and not Bob. You see, well, Bob's a bit of a flirt away from work, and he's got a great sense of humor, but he's always treated the women around the office very respectfully. He's always been friendly, but very professional," Laura stated. "I've never heard any gossip or rumors about him being involved with anybody at work, and with his looks and his personality, you know there must have been several women along the way who have tried to snare him. I know of at least three."

"Sure. But did any of those women get naked and blush a lot?" Kate asked her. "That's what got him interested in me. It can be a very effective way to get a man's interest."

"If I were still single, I'd keep it in mind."

"Worked like a charm for me." Kate was smiling. "And I wasn't even trying."

Laura parked the car and they went into an Italian restaurant.

As soon as they were seated, Laura asked, "Did it go farther yesterday than just kissing?" Laura studied Kate's face, and noted another sudden flush. "It did! Good girl. I knew you had it in you."

"It didn't go *that* far." Kate watched Laura's eyes widen at the double entendre before she put an end to the discussion of her love life. "Now. About work, who's a suspect?"

There was a pause as they studied their menus briefly. A waitress walked over and they both ordered chef salads and iced tea.

"Everyone," Laura continued as if there had not been a pause. "They've all been here when money was missing. It's hard to see how any of them could have done it. The shortages don't have anything to do with payroll, and of course, the bank reconciliations and accounts receivable books always balance out. The only two areas where there have been unusual discrepancies are in accounts payable and cash receipts. The shortages usually seem to appear when a new girl has been on the job for about a week and a half."

The waitress brought their food and left. Laura continued talking as she squeezed lemon and stirred some sugar into her iced tea. "I have a feeling this time it's going to be sooner though, because we took so long bringing you on board. I think whoever is stealing the money must need it pretty badly by now."

"Have you tried marked bills? Hidden cameras? Or drug testing?" Kate suggested. "This could very well be drug related."

"I don't know about marked bills, we can ask the Loss Prevention people about that idea, and I think it would be hard to install hidden cameras without alerting the guilty party. I'll ask about that, too. Remember, all the employees passed a drug screening test when they were first hired, and we haven't seen any behavior from anyone suggesting that we need to retest one of them." Laura put butter on a roll and ate a bite before she went on. "We'd hate to put everyone through another drug test if we don't have to. Besides if we do that, we'll definitely warn the thief that we're looking."

"But it's gone on so long," Kate protested, "surely the guilty person must know you're onto the thefts."

"Well, the first time it happened, Bob and I thought it was the new girl we had just hired. Luckily, she was not a very good worker so we just let her go while she was still on probation. The next time it happened, we were sure it wasn't the new girl. So when her husband was offered a new job in Houston, we transferred her to our Houston office. There hasn't been any sign of embezzlement in Texas." Laura paused. "The people in our local office were told she'd been sent back to the agency."

The waitress came over to refill their iced tea and see if they needed anything else. Although they hadn't finished their salads because they were talking, they both ordered warm apple pie. They focused on eating for a few minutes so that they would be finished with the salads by the time the waitress brought their pies.

Laura continued, "The third time we were completely convinced the thief wasn't the girl but she was the one we mentioned that was having a rough pregnancy. So, we are letting her work at home on some special projects and using a little creative bookkeeping to keep her on the payroll and covered by insurance. Actually, she's going to do most of the Accounts Payable work for us. That way she will help free you up to do your investigation. That is top secret too, of course."

"If she's doing the work, why is so much of it piled up?" Kate asked, filled with curiosity. "Payables is a mess."

"Two reasons. First, she's been sick a lot lately, and second, we didn't want her to do too much until we had someone sitting at your desk. Otherwise, it would look suspicious." Laura smiled. "I mean, why hire anyone if the work is all caught up? And who could be doing it? I doubt if anyone would believe we had elves coming in and doing AP at night."

"What about the fourth girl?" Kate managed between bites.

"She was a temp, a very good one, so we fixed her up with another company. She wound up earning more money and working closer to her home. Once we figured out the temps were being blamed for something that someone else was doing we tried to make sure that none of them were hurt. That's one thing about Bob, instead of that cold corporate mentality, he cared enough to try to make things right. Most bosses would just let the girls go without worrying about them. These girls never knew they were suspected of theft. They were spared that embarrassment." Laura looked Kate straight in the eye. "Now this time we'll handle it a little bit differently. This time we will make it seem like you are under suspicion."

"Even as a ploy, that's going to be hard." Kate wasn't looking forward to being accused. "Emotionally, I mean."

"If you need to talk to either Bob or myself, call us at home." Laura gave Kate Bob's home number, adding innocently, "And you already know where he lives. Personally, I think the biggest strain is going to be on all of our acting skills."

The waitress brought their check and Laura paid it. "We'd better get back to work."

"Aw gee, do we have to?" Kate protested jokingly.

"No, but remember, Bob's there," Laura bribed.

"Okay, I'm ready." Kate rushed for the car, laughing.

Laura settled in the car then got serious for a minute. "After Joe, I thought you never would be, ready for someone, I mean." She started to drive back to the office.

Kate's husband, Joe, had been hit by a drunk driver coming home late from work one night. At the time, Suzy and Sarah were eighteen months old, and Sam was three and a half.

It had taken about a year and a half, but Kate knew she was ready to get back to living again. She smiled to herself; it's just that she wasn't sure she was ready to fall head over heels in love again, and she was also partially afraid that's exactly what was happening to her.

"I'll never stop loving Joe, but I will go on with my life," Kate replied with quiet dignity.

"Because Joe would want it that way?" Laura asked.

"Partly, as cliché as that sounds. It's also partly because I believe that if I live my life to the fullest and have my own interests, I'll be a better mother to my kids. I wouldn't want to wind up a bitter old hag. And, last but not least, for myself." She smiled, "Life's too short not to fully enjoy it."

"So how serious is it between you and Bob?" Laura quizzed her.

"Well, it's way too soon to be sure, but I have a sneaking suspicion this could turn out to be major. The real thing." Kate was suddenly very quiet, then finally she added, "It's almost frightening the way I feel about him; after all, I only met him yesterday."

"I remember that you fell in love with Joe almost the instant you met him. I swear I heard a click," Laura smiled, remembering, "sort of like the click I heard yesterday, when you looked up and met Bob's eyes."

"It wasn't his eyes I met yesterday when I looked up." Kate laughed, flushing.

Laura parked the car. "Not then, you silly goose. In the pool, when we were tackling Jack. At one point in the game, you and Bob looked at each other and almost made the water boil."

"I remember." Kate laughed. "And you, my dear friend, notice too darn much. Let's get out of my love life and go back to work."

Shortly after lunch, Kate got a call from her mother. "I have a wonderful idea, dear," she exclaimed. "Why don't I come to your house to sit for the kids? That way you wouldn't have to work so hard to get them fed and dressed and over to my house, while you're getting ready for work."

"Gee, Mom, why didn't I think of that?" Kate had brought up the same idea before, but her mother insisted on having the kids brought over to her house.

"I don't know, dear, but it's going to be great." She gave a sly little laugh. "And then *your* house will be the one that looks like a tornado hit it."

"Golly, that *will* be great, thanks Mom." Kate hung up laughing.

The rest of the afternoon passed without incident. Kate buried herself in her work. She made a sizable dent in the backed up stack of invoices in Accounts Payable, then she made a list of the type of reports she would like to begin studying from all the other desks. She gave her list to Laura, who said she would arrange for Bob to get the records to her.

She only met one other co-worker that day, Jerry Weisner, a tall, friendly man who was in charge of the purchasing department. He came into her office and introduced himself. He gave her a list of some of his special vendors, vendors that had unusual terms or ways of doing business.

He sat on the corner of her desk, and tried to give her the insight on some of the things that were peculiar to this company. He had black hair, brown eyes and an easy, relaxed manner that was matched by his attire of comfortable jeans and a well-worn green polo shirt.

Just as Jerry was about to leave her office, he smiled at her and remarked sadly, "I don't know if you're going to make it around here."

"Why not?" Kate was indignant. "What's wrong with me?"

"You're dressed way too formally, and we're a pretty relaxed group." He smiled at her. "You'll have to loosen up and wear something a lot more casual or you'll make the rest of us peons look bad."

"Okay, I will." She had already realized that she was way overdressed for this particular office. She smiled at him. "I promise to be casual in the future but I had to try to make a good impression on my first day. You can't blame a girl for that."

"When I talked to Bob earlier, I got the feeling he was impressed." Jerry smiled. "Tomorrow, wear tight jeans and you'll knock him off his feet."

Kate was shocked; did her infatuation show? "Do I want to knock him off his feet?"

"Why not? It couldn't hurt." Jerry waved a hand at her as he left.

Kate went back to work. She barely saw either Laura or Bob until it was time to leave, except for one time when she was at the water cooler and saw Bob coming out of his office.

She heard Laura whisper in her ear. "Careful! You're making the water boil again."

She was cleaning off her desk when Bob walked into her cubicle. "So, how was your first day?"

"Well, this is a simple job but there is something that I can't quite put my hands on," Kate answered. "I think it may be very hard for me trying to picture one of these women as a thief. They all seem so normal, very friendly and helpful."

"Forget the co-workers. How about the boss?" Bob prodded as he looked out to see if anyone was nearby and began to move around her desk towards her. "Is he nice?"

"The ogre?" Kate teased, backing off. "I hardly saw him all day."

"Ogre?" Bob pretended to be insulted, moving away, back towards the opening of the cubicle. "I heard he was a pretty nice guy. All the other ladies seem to like him."

"No accounting for taste." Coolly, she raised an eyebrow. "Well, I'm out of here." She picked up her purse and threw it onto her shoulder.

Bob took her arm and gently but firmly led her back to his office. He shut his office door and leaned against it. "Not so fast, come here. I haven't kissed you all day."

Kate felt her heart jump in her chest while she looked up at Bob with wide eyes.

"In the office? Isn't that called sexual harassment?" Kate grinned at him. "Didn't we talk about that last night?"

"Only if it makes working conditions hard on you," Bob winked, "and that's not what I had in mind."

"What's it called if I make it hard on you?" Kate asked, with exaggerated innocence.

"That's called arousal." He caught Kate in his arms and began to kiss her. "And I think you're guilty of it already," he managed between kisses.

"God, I hope so," Kate whispered back, also between tender kisses, "because you're guilty of it too." She managed to pull away. "We shouldn't do this here; if we do, sooner or later we'll get caught."

"You're right. I don't like it, but you're right." Bob gave Kate one long, wet passionate kiss and then pulled back leaving Kate feeling strangely rejected.

"You don't have to agree so easily," Kate complained, straightening her hair and lipstick before they left the office.

"Don't worry, you're not going to get rid of me so quickly," he promised.

"Bob?" Kate said as they walked across the parking lot, "How could I get hold of some of the older financial reports to try and trace the lost money?"

"I'll make copies and bring them to your house," he offered. "But make sure you don't work too much on them at home. Of course, I'll pay you extra for the homework."

"Is this just an excuse to come over to my house?" Kate asked, her head tilted to one side.

"Well, it works, doesn't it?" Bob smiled. "But who needs an excuse?"

"Truthfully?" She met his eyes. "You don't, consider this a standing invitation to come over anytime. The kids are in bed by eight," Kate offered, grinning wickedly.

"Why did I ever think you were shy?" Bob was a little

overwhelmed.

"It was probably those blushes, fools 'em every time," Kate teased, "but don't get too carried away. I have three built-in chaperones, remember?"

"How could I forget?" He grinned.

"And the kids aren't your biggest obstacles either," she said mysteriously.

"What do you mean?" He was dubious. "Are there any other obstacles between us?"

"You'll find out." She winked and gave him a saucy grin. "Later."

She got into her van and drove off, leaving him standing there puzzled.

Chapter Four

Later that evening Kate waited for her doorbell to ring. She was hopeful that Bob would arrive at any moment, so she used the nervous energy to get some things done. The minute she got home from work, she'd thrown on her old grubby clothes, then played with the kids and dogs for a while before fixing dinner. Then, she put the kids to bed and the dogs out, and quickly picked up the living room, dusting and rearranging the small colorful throw pillows on her plain brown sofa. She cleaned the kitchen and put a bottle of California Chablis in the refrigerator. Then she cleaned the downstairs bathroom.

Finally she'd taken a quick shower and changed again. She dressed carefully, although with a somewhat casual deception, in her best emerald green blouse and crisp white shorts. She let her long, auburn hair out of the severe bun she'd worn it in at work and brushed it until it fell in soft waves down her back.

She stood back and surveyed the living room objectively. It looked cozy and inviting. She had made up for her plain, worn furniture by filling the room with personal touches. The walls were painted a very light earth tone, and most of the furniture was in shades of brown, ranging from tan to chocolate. It could have been too dark, but she had thrown in lots of colorful accents, brightly colored throw pillows and a hand knitted afghan draped on the back of the sofa. The walls had several pictures of her kids and a group of antique mirrors. She also had several hanging plants and knickknacks on every end table. .

By 9:30 she was ready. It was the most excited she'd been since her husband died. Finally, there was a knock at the door. Her heart seemed to be racing as she went to open it. It wasn't

Bob. She felt the excitement drain out of her as she opened the door and found the rude, obnoxious jerk who lived next door standing on her porch.

"Hi Tim." She managed to get out the greeting without showing too much disappointment. "What do you want?"

"From you doll? Everything I can get!" He smirked, eyeballing her tight shorts. "But for now, can I use your car to give mine a jump-start? I need to go to the store and I've got a dead battery."

"Sure, Tim, no problem. Let me get my keys." She reached for her purse and rummaged for her car keys.

She was relieved, for once, it didn't sound like he was going to try to stay and make a pest out of himself. She handed him her car keys.

"You wouldn't happen to have any beer, would ya, doll?" he asked, as his eyes made their way up to her chest, looking her at breasts with a leer. "If you did I could stay here with you instead of going out. You look good enough to-"

Just then Bob walked up behind them. He took one look at Kate's face with the frozen smile and knew that the other man wasn't welcome.

"Hi Kate. Am I interrupting anything?" Bob asked casually as he reached out to pull her into a warm hug. He had replaced his office attire with jeans and a soft, clean white T-shirt.

He let his eyes wander from Kate just long enough to take in the beer belly and the dirty, grease stained T-shirt worn by the man on the porch.

"Hi, darling. I'm sorry, Tim. I'm out of beer, and as you can see I have company," she said firmly. Then she reached up and lightly stroked Bob's freshly shaven cheek.

"But I was here first!" Tim protested loudly, sounding like a petulant child.

"You came here uninvited, claiming that you had car trouble. Go. Jump start your car and bring back my car keys, then Bob and I would like to be alone." She kept her voice firm and low but still commanding.

As soon as Tim went out to move her van, Bob stepped into her living room, shut the door, and pulled her into his arms and greeted her with a long, passionate kiss.

"Darling?" Bob looked amused. "I like it, but was that for my benefit or his?"

"For his," she grinned at him, "but this is just for you."

She snaked an arm around his neck and returned his kiss.

When the kiss broke, Bob said, "I'm going out to help get him on his way."

"He can't be gone soon enough for me." Kate smiled, "Hurry back in, okay?"

Bob went out to Kate's van, which Tim had driven far enough to align her front bumper up with his. Bob helped Tim get his old battered pick-up started and returned to Kate's house with her car keys. When he returned in just a few minutes, Kate was waiting for him at the door. She had soft music playing in the background, and had opened the bottle of wine.

"I thought you'd never get here," she said, hugging him warmly.

"Oh, is that why you were entertaining another man?" he teased as he returned the hug, running his hands up and down her back.

"That's not a man, that's my neighbor." She handed him a glass of wine and gestured to the sofa, grimacing. "A lower life form."

"He wants you." Bob sat down on the sofa and sipped his wine.

She sat on the sofa next to Bob and looked him straight in his eyes. "He's not going to get me."

"Good!" He reached out and pulled her gently into his strong arms. "I want you, too." He kissed her with enough passion to send shivers down her spine.

Kate pulled back and met his eyes for a long breathless moment. Finally she spoke in a soft, but steady voice. "It's still pretty soon, remember we just met yesterday." She leaned forward to kiss him gently. "I'm a little surprised that I feel so much for you. I thought those feelings had died in me when I lost Joe. I mean, I knew somewhere in the back of my mind that I'd find somebody way off in the future. It's just that it's a little strange, almost scary, that the future seems to have come so fast. I not only haven't been to bed with anyone since my husband died, I haven't even gone out on a date with anyone."

"I don't want to rush you." Bob gently ran his hand up her neck and caressed her cheek, laughing suddenly, "Hell, I do want to rush you, but not against your will, if you can understand that?"

"I understand. The thing is, I want you, too." She smiled and rubbed her cheek into his palm almost purring like a kitten. She savored the feel of his hand on her face. "But I want to enjoy the feelings I have for a while, instead of acting on them so quickly. And I want to get to know you better. Does that make any sense?"

"Of course it makes sense, anticipation and all that." He trailed baby kisses down her throat.

He leaned back on the sofa, pulling her down on top of him; he ran his big hands through her hair and pulled her face down to his. He kissed her, starting gently and building up until the passion washed over them both, like waves crashing onto the shore. His hands slid under her blouse, pulling it free from her shorts, and he used his fingers to gently stroke and tease her breasts. She returned the favor, running her hands inside his T-shirt that he wore loose, not tucked into his jeans.

Finally, he broke off the kiss, breathing heavily. He held her firmly and tenderly, nuzzling her hair and bringing his breathing under control. Gradually the sound of the phone ringing penetrated her dazed senses.

She pulled back slightly and said, "I'll let the machine get that."

A whining voice came over the air; it was her neighbor Tim. "I know you have company over there, Sweet cheeks, but you'd better bring those dogs in before I go outside and stop their barking, and I mean permanently."

"What a jerk!" Bob was indignant. "How can he talk to you like that?"

"A jerk, that he is. Well, I guess we've been saved by the bell. I've always hated that stupid expression." She was angry at the interruption and still panting with arousal.

"Let's just say I don't think 'saved' is the word I would use, but he is sure one heck of a mood killer." Bob grinned ruefully. "But since we agreed to wait, he probably called at just the right time. Unfortunately."

"One of these days, I'm going to have to do something about him, something violent, painful and terribly wicked, but not right now. Do you want any more wine?" When he shook his head no, Kate pulled her blouse back into place and then picked up the wineglasses to carry them into the kitchen. "Remember when I said the kids weren't the biggest obstacles you faced? Well, you're about to meet your obstacles. You'd better pull your shirt back down, or you'll get little doggie scratches all over your body because my beasties are not well-mannered." She grinned a little devilishly and continued, "It might help to umm, cross your legs, too. They've been known to jump into men's laps, and land rather painfully on certain parts of their anatomy."

He barely had his shirt in place when two small Boston terriers came in and leaped into his lap, jumping up and down, wiggling and trying to lick him all over.

Kate came back in. "Bob, meet Teddy and Charger. They'll settle down in about a century or two, when they've finished greeting you"

"They're a little overwhelming, aren't they?" He was laughing as he tried to avoid little doggie tongues and toenails. The worst part was the eight doggie feet, all of which seemed to be excitedly jumping up and down on his crotch.

"Yes, but in a while they'll go up to the kids' rooms," she told him.

"How can two dogs seem like a herd?" Bob asked her laughing, petting the two small black and white dynamos, while still fending off doggie kisses.

"The word is 'pack' and this is no pack yet, but Teddy's pregnant so it really will be in a couple of weeks," she laughed, walking into the kitchen.

"Great." Bob really seemed to enjoy the attention from the two wiggling bundles of energy, but he couldn't help teasing her gently. "You need more dogs, really." There was a hint of mischief in his voice.

The two dogs eventually settled down enough to leave Bob and disappear up the stairs, heading for the kids' bedrooms. When Bob went into the kitchen to find Kate, she was bending over with her head in the refrigerator, putting the wine away. He walked up behind her and gave her a smart pat on her firm behind.

"You have such a great behind, I couldn't resist." He nuzzled her neck, whispering, "And, I probably never will."

"You've got great buns, too." Kate made a great show of facing him as she moved around him in the small kitchen, making sure he could not get to her backside again, and being very obvious about it. Finally, she relented and put her arms around his waist. Slowly she slid one hand down to his behind and quickly pinched his backside.

"I prefer to goose yours." She kissed him. "Remember when I said it was too soon?"

"Anticipation?" he murmured between kisses.

"Well, that was at least three hours ago," she sighed as the waves of sensation filled her senses.

The hand that had pinched him stayed where it was; only now it was stroking his buttocks. Bob pulled back and looked at her speculatively.

Finally he said, "As much as I hate to say it, it's still too soon, for what seems to be building between us." He kissed her quickly. "I'd better go."

"You're right, but I don't like it very much." She returned the kiss. "See you tomorrow."

"Goodnight." He kissed her again and started towards the door.

"Bob?" She stopped him. "What about the papers you were bringing over? You never brought them in."

"I'll bring them to you tomorrow. It's too late for you to do any work on them tonight." He kissed her one more time.

"No, bring them in now. I won't work on them for very long, but I think I need something good and boring to help me get to sleep. And you don't need any excuse to come over tomorrow, if you want," she teased him. "Just call first to make sure I've kicked Tim out."

"Oh, I think it would be safe to come over without calling. Tim and I have an understanding," he said, raising one eyebrow.

"What did you do?" She looked up at him.

"I just let him know that this claim has been staked, and the boundaries marked, so to speak." Bob kissed her nose.

"Charming. Now, I feel like an old gold mine." She sounded annoyed.

"You're much more precious than mere gold." He gave her a twisted little grin.

"Do you have any Irish ancestors, Bob?" She smiled at him. "Because that sounds like blarney to me."

"It's the truth, my love." Bob went out and brought the papers in from his car. "Just don't try to do too much tonight, okay?"

"I won't. I do have one idea though. That girl who's

working at home? The pregnant one?" She stayed in his arms, snuggling.

"Shelly?" Bob supplied the name. "What about her?"

"Could we enlist her to help us? It would probably be easier for her to look into some things at home than for me to do it at the office. I mean, it's a little out of my department to go over things like register tapes from the stores, or cash room reports. And it's more difficult for her to do Accounts Payable work at home. If I'm doing AP at the office, things would seem normal, and if she's busy looking for discrepancies at home, no one will know about it. What do you think?"

"I think it's a good idea, but I still want you in charge of looking for the thefts for two reasons. First, she was never told about the missing money and second, she has no auditing experience. But I will call her and explain how she can help you, and tell her to follow your lead." He kissed her. "And then I'll have her email or call you and you two can work out the details. Okay?"

Kate nodded, still cuddled in his arms.

"Now, I'd really better get going. Goodnight, Kate."

"Goodnight, boss." After she gave him one last long, passionate kiss, she reluctantly let him go.

The rest of the week went on much the same. Kate and Bob worked together efficiently at the office during the day, and kissed each other senseless on her sofa at night. Anticipation was growing to a point just slightly beyond torture, but it was such a delicious torture that they still waited. On Thursday, Kate told Bob that they were invited to have Sunday dinner with Joe's mother.

"Won't I be out of place?" Bob felt a little intimidated when he thought about meeting her late husband's mother. "Won't she resent me?"

He was not only feeling a little odd about meeting Joe's mother but he also couldn't forget Laura's reservations about the woman. He vaguely wondered if his manners would pass the test.

"No, Ida especially wants you to come with us. I don't even know how she heard about you, but she has and she wants to meet you," Kate pleaded. "She's mellowed out since Laura saw her last. She's put her grief behind her and gotten active again. She's back to how she used to be, fun and full of the devil. She's finally made a new life for herself. She even has a new beau now and he's really stirred her up. In fact, since she found George, she's been nagging me to get out and find someone. She's almost as much of a matchmaker as Laura." Kate paused. "Her only fear is that if I find someone else to share my life with, she'll be left out. I would never do that to her, she will always be my kids' grandma. Please come, she's really a neat lady, and she's a big part of our lives."

"Okay, I'll go." He was still a little unsure about the whole idea. "If she's important to you then she'll be important to me, too."

When Bob came over Friday night, they greeted each other with a few passionate kisses and then cuddled up on the sofa and talked about themselves. Just talking for a long time. They talked about their marriages and their childhoods. He told Kate about his messy divorce, and she told him about the terrible phone call informing her that Joe had been killed. They even told each other some of the adventures Laura had gotten them both into.

Bob's favorite story was about the time some woman's husband rode his small motorcycle into the ladies' restroom at a campground and bellowed for the woman to come out of the stall. The man had been just a little under the influence at the time. The best part was when Kate and Laura had snuck up behind him and blocked the restroom doors shut from the outside.

"You should have seen the park ranger's face when he found

a man, his wife, and a motorcycle in the women's room in the morning," Kate smiled, remembering the scene. "The poor guy was lucky he didn't get arrested."

"I'll bet you and Laura came to his defense," Bob told her with a laugh. "After all, you two were the ones who trapped him in the rest room."

"Of course we stood up for him," Kate grinned slyly, "to this day, the poor guy doesn't really know how he came to be stuck in a ladies room. Even Joe and Jack never knew who actually blocked the restroom door shut."

"I'll bet they guessed," Bob grinned.

"I'm sure they did," she grinned back, "anyway, I learned all my tricks from Laura."

The conversation was a departure for them. Up to this point, they either discussed work or got sidetracked by their physical attraction for each other. This was the first time they really talked, the first time they really opened up to each other. Before the conversation ended, they had touched lightly on dreams and ambitions. The conversation lasted for quite a while, right up until the clock struck midnight. It was the time Bob usually left.

"Remember anticipation?" Bob asked.

"Somehow, I feel it's still too soon," Kate said softly, "but the right time is coming."

"We're not kids," Bob said, "we'll know when the time is right."

He kissed her again, she slid her hands under the hem of his polo shirt, and he sat up long enough to take it off then he lay back down on top of her. He began to kiss her with a passion that left them both gasping and breathless. Kate was conscious of feeling proof of Bob's arousal pressing up against her. Still, he held back, controlling himself. He held her gently and stroked her hair with so much tenderness it left her breathless. Finally, reluctantly, he sat up and slowly regained his poise.

He pulled his shirt back on, breathing deeply. He stood up

and leaned over to kiss her gently on the forehead, her soft neck and finally her lips before walking to the door. When he reached the door, he glanced back at her. She was still reclining, her mouth red and swollen from his kisses, and gazing at him with wide green eyes.

"Man! What an erotic picture you make, I don't want to leave but I have to." He stopped her as she started to open her mouth to say something. "Tomorrow, we'll do something fun with the kids. I have a feeling it's going to be very important for me to get to know them, and for them to get to know me."

Kate and Bob spent Saturday together with the kids. They took the little ones shopping, stopped for burgers, and then treated the trio to a matinee. There was only a minor squabble over which movie to see, but they settled on the latest Disney cartoon. Armed with popcorn, cokes and bon bons, they laughed at the hero's antics.

After the movie, they went swimming in Bob's pool. By nap time, all three kids were tired and cranky, so naturally they gave Kate a hard time, arguing with her when she tried to get them to take their afternoon naps. After quelling the minor rebellion, she joined Bob in his den, cuddling up on the sofa with him.

"They're having a great time with you," Kate told Bob, kissing his neck. "You're wonderful with them. It almost feels like we're a real family."

"They're really great kids, Kate." He kissed her. "I've enjoyed every minute I've spent with them, except for when I wanted to have you alone."

Indeed, it felt so much like they were a real family that later as they all watched videos, Kate looked at Bob stretched out on the floor with the kids and felt a strange tightness in her chest. It was a strange, mixed emotion; for one thing she still missed Joe. She deeply regretted that he never really had a chance to play with the kids, or just lie on the floor with them like that. On the other hand, she was delighted that Bob was so good with them. The kids really liked him, too. It brought home to Kate just how much they needed to have a man in their lives.

After dinner, Bob took her home and kissed her good-bye at the door. He realized that Kate needed to have some time to spend alone with her kids.

"What time should I pick you up tomorrow?" he asked her. "Are we still going to your mother-in-law's for lunch?"

"Come over around eleven." She leaned into his kiss.

"What should I wear? I want to make a good impression," he asked.

"We'll be in our casual clothes, shorts and T-shirts. I may even wear a sundress." She nuzzled his neck.

He looked into her eyes, first putting a finger under her chin and gently pulling her face up to his. "Do me a favor? Wear the yellow sundress you wore last Sunday at my house. That low-cut, backless, sexy as hell sundress. Please."

She met his eyes and almost forgot to breathe. "Yes. Sure, anything you say." Suddenly she heard herself and she grinned impishly, "Maybe."

He removed his finger from under her chin and put one hand on each shoulder. Slowly he slid his hands down her back, lower and lower, until finally he was cupping her buttocks. With a quick movement he pulled her against himself. Her eyes widened as she felt the hardness pressing against her.

Softly he said one word, "Please."

"Sir, you fight dirty." She kissed him deeply and stepped quickly back. "I'll wear the dress, but don't expect to get your way that easy every time."

To Bob's surprise, Sunday dinner turned out to be fun. Joe's mother, Ida, was definitely not a typical grandmother, whatever that is these days. Like Kate, she had a Boston terrier dog. Unlike Kate's dogs though, hers was older and more sedate.

Ida was late getting home from her exercise class, and drove up at the same time they did. She jumped out of her car, which turned out to be a classic red T-bird, Bob noted with surprise. She wore a bright purple jogging suit. Ida was about sixty, very tiny and full of spirit. She hugged the kids with joy and laughter on her face, then turned and hugged Kate the same way.

"You must be Bob." She turned to greet him, sticking out her hand for him to shake. "I'm so pleased to meet you."

"I'm pleased to meet you, too. I've heard so much about you from Kate." Bob relaxed as he realized that Ida did indeed, accept him.

Kate had to ask, "Ida, how did you hear about Bob? I haven't even told my folks about him, yet."

"I called you at the office and your line was busy, so I asked for Laura," she smiled ruefully. "I had put off apologizing to her for far too long. She and I had quite a fight when I got so obsessive after losing my husband and Joe. You know Laura, she's so straightforward, she tried to tell me I was taking over your family as a substitute for mine. She was right, but at the time, I couldn't see it."

"You've gotten past that now." Kate slid her arm around her mother-in-law's shoulder.

"And Laura helped. I just didn't want to face it." Ida smiled, "I told Laura that she did the right thing, shaking me up like that. I had to find a whole new life. Now it looks like you're ready to do the same thing."

"I want you to know that wherever my new life takes me, you'll always be part of it. You'll always be family." Kate hugged Ida again.

Ida fixed dinner by ordering in for pizza, explaining that the reason she went to exercise classes was so she could have things like pizza when she wanted them. While waiting for the pizza, she quickly made dessert. It was a chocolate custard baked with a cloud of meringue on top. No piecrust.

When Kate asked Ida about that, Ida just grinned.

"If I remember right, you hate rolling out piecrust," Kate

teased.

"Got me," Ida conceded.

The meringue was piled high on top of the chocolate custard and browned nicely. The servings were all jumbled up in the dishes, but the concoction tasted surprisingly good.

Just in time for dessert, Ida's new boyfriend, George, came over. He was a jolly, plump man of about sixty-five. He promptly challenged Bob to a game of golf the next weekend, and played 'horsey' with the kids on the floor. It was a game that quickly disintegrated into a wrestling match. Ida, the person Laura said was so strict and stuffy, was the referee of the wrestling match and served seconds of dessert to the winners.

Kate whispered to Bob, "I think George really loosened her up, don't you?"

George, who overheard, said, "Loosened her up? Kate! I damned near unhinged her!" He grabbed Kate in a big hug.

Shortly before they left, Ida took Bob aside and told him that she was glad to see Kate with someone, finally. Bob was relieved to hear that she felt that way, instead of resenting him and his place in Kate's life.

"I know Kate loved Joe, but I don't want her to be alone forever." She said quietly, "I want my grandchildren to have a stepfather, too."

"Well, it's a little too soon to think about that." Bob smiled at the tiny, gray-haired woman. "But it's nice to know that if things work out between Kate and myself, you'll be happy about it. I know Kate thinks the world of you." He hugged her gently. "And now I know why."

Walking to the car, Bob was very pleased with himself. "She likes me!"

"Yes, she does, but Bob," Kate teased, "she likes all men. I've never seen it fail yet, except for Tim, my next door neighbor."

"Well, at least I beat him." Bob grinned, "That's something.

Just wait until you're in the same position."

"What do you mean?" She was puzzled.

Bob gave her a devilish grin. "Wait until my mother compares you to my ex-wife." He laughed at her surprised expression. "Hey, don't worry, if you're breathing, you've already won the contest."

"That's good, I'm sure I can remember how to breathe," Kate raised her mouth to his for a quick kiss, "as long as I don't look into your eyes."

Chapter Five

Kate's second week on the job was much the same as the first week. Once again Kate and Bob worked hard at the office, then spent the evenings together. The only change was that this week they finally started to do a little work in the evenings instead of spending the whole time entwined in each other's arms on the sofa.

Monday night, they sat at the kitchen table poring over various accounting reports trying to find clues to the missing money. They focused on trying to trace the cash receipts from the very moment a sale was rung up at the retail store to the time it was deposited into the bank. They found some small discrepancies, which Kate would research in more depth at a later time, but nothing that was nearly enough to explain the majority of the missing money. Finally, disgusted with digging into a year's worth of boring reports, Kate looked over at Bob.

"Are we getting bored with each other already?" Kate teased him, "Here we are, acting just like two mature adults should, working at the kitchen table."

"Well, it seems safer than what I'd like to do at the kitchen table." He got up and walked over to the coffee maker, refreshing his cup and pouring her one. "Work is definitely my second choice."

He grabbed her hair, none too gently but without causing Kate any pain, and pulled her head back for a long, deep kiss. "It might even be my third choice."

"Enough work. Let's take this coffee into the living room and rearrange your priorities." She stood up and took his hand, leading him to the sofa.

Once they sat down and curled up in each other's arms, however, talk returned to the problems at work. Shelly, the pregnant girl who working from home, had been a big help. Over the phone, she and Kate had discussed and investigated several things. Even though they had not met yet, Shelly and Kate were following a couple of interesting trails.

Cuddled with Bob, Kate filled him in on the progress and where their investigation was headed. The thefts always started off small but soon the amounts went up to several hundred dollars at a time. Sometimes thousands. As far as Kate could tell the total amount stolen was far over one hundred thousand dollars.

As they talked, Kate's hand made little forays on Bob's neck, and Bob idly stroked her arm. Eventually, all talk ended, and the kisses began. Warm, wonderful, romantic kisses with soft touches and erotic cuddling. Before things went too far, Bob reluctantly went home.

Tuesday, Kate had a long meeting with Jerry from Purchasing. They discussed ways to make things run smoother between their respective departments. The company was changing over to a new computer program that would provide more extensive Accounts Payable reports and would mesh perfectly with the output from the Purchasing Department. After the meeting, Jerry took her to lunch.

Jerry proved to be a great lunch companion. He was an expressive talker and he kept her laughing at his jokes and stories. The only quiet moment during lunch came when he talked about his wife.

"I'm married to the most gorgeous woman alive and she's as sweet as she is beautiful," he bragged, with sadness in his eyes.

"Jerry, what's wrong?" Kate asked gently. "I can tell something's troubling you."

"Oh, it's nothing terrible," he told her, smiling again, "it's just that lately she hasn't been well. Nothing serious, but still. . ."

"If I can help let me know," Kate told him.

"I will," Jerry said as they left the restaurant. "Thanks Kate. I sure hope they keep you as a permanent employee."

"Me too, I really like this job," she said with a grin. "And the people are great."

Tuesday night, Bob reminded Kate that she was supposed to be late or stay home occasionally to build up a record of poor attendance and tardiness.

"I don't want you wearing yourself out, working every night after I leave, and I know you do." He was concerned for her. "Stay home now and then. Remember, your poor attendance record will make it easier to accuse you. We might even get lucky and have the thief try to throw suspicion on you when you're not there."

"Bob," she cuddled up with him, nibbling on his neck, "if I stay home, I won't get to see you all day. I'll miss you. And remember, I want to put off building a poor attendance record until the puppies are born. I'll have the worst attendance record you ever saw, starting as soon as Teddy whelps. She's due on Friday. I'm going to have a litter of puppies to care for, remember?"

"The herd," Bob gave an exaggerated groan, then he relented, "I can't wait to see them, they'll be cute as hell."

Kate arrived at work over an hour late Wednesday morning. Immediately, Bob locked her in his office and gave her a severe tongue-lashing. Between moments of yelling loud enough to be heard through the office door, he was nibbling her neck and kissing her passionately; his tongue ravaging her mouth.

Kate was aware of something different in his kisses, a feeling of tension in him, a sense that he was holding something back. She couldn't put her finger on exactly what it was. She wasn't thinking very well, she was too swept away by the delicious sensations his mouth was causing as he nibbled his way down her neck.

Whatever his problem was, it was not lack of passion. She was in his office for quite a long time and her face was flushed and she was breathing heavily when she finally emerged.

"Wow!" Rita, a large motherly woman, came running over. "I never heard him get so mad before." She put her arms around Kate in a friendly, sympathetic hug.

"I guess I deserved it." Kate fought to hide her smile. "I was awfully late. I should have called him to explain."

Laura came over. "Back to work, Rita. If you've finished the payroll, I'm sure I can find some other work for you to do. Remember, we're getting ready for a tax audit. Kate, I want to see you in my office. Now." She held her office door open for Kate to go in.

Rita's face turned dark red and she sputtered indignantly, "But . . . but Bob already yelled at her!"

"Go on, Rita. I won't be too rough on her. I promise." Laura softened her voice. "No yelling."

Rita turned and started to stalk away. After she had taken about a half dozen steps, she turned back. "Just don't pick on her, Laura, you hear me? This place is getting so bad I may have to start sending out my resume." She stormed away.

As soon as Laura got Kate into her office, she shut the door and they burst out laughing. They almost choked trying not to make too much noise.

"I've never told Rita to get back to work before. Did you see her face? I thought she'd go into shock," Laura managed to get out. She was hugging her sides, holding her laughter in.

"I was almost afraid she'd have a heart attack, and I felt responsible. She was only being protective of me." Kate shook her head. "She felt really sorry for me because I was getting yelled at."

"As if you needed any sympathy." Laura smiled mischievously. "Unless I miss my guess, there was very little yelling going on in that office."

"Well, you're wrong. I got a severe tongue-lashing. At least," Kate grinned and winked, "he had his tongue all over me."

"Ah, that's where you got that glow." Laura sat down, her voice taking on a serious edge. "But I do need to talk to you."

"What's up?" Kate sat down.

"There was a thousand dollars missing from the checking account as of yesterday, and it can be traced directly to you." She was all business now. "Well, to Accounts Payable."

"What area of payables? How was the check coded? Was it for a parts purchase? Or for office supplies? Rent?" Kate asked, instantly alert.

"It was coded as a parts purchase, but Jerry doesn't have a purchase order to match it, and the address it was supposed to be mailed to is not the address of any of our vendors. It was also a handwritten check, not computer generated." Laura was grim.

"So it begins?" Kate asked quietly.

"Yes. You'll be accused of theft tomorrow, just loudly enough so everyone will know about it," Laura replied.

"I still don't like the idea," Kate moaned. "It makes me feel almost sick to my stomach."

"Just remember that it's all an act. Bob and I have complete faith in you," Laura said gently, "and we're on your side."

"I know. I just hope it helps to catch the thief. I like all my co-workers but this has got to stop." Kate became pensive, "I just hate the idea of any of these people getting themselves into trouble."

"Look at the bright side." Laura grinned, "You'll get to spend a long time in Bob's office with the door shut."

"More tongue-lashings?" Returning her grin Kate said, "I could get used to that."

That night, Bob came over again. He didn't bring any office files with him and he definitely did not have work in mind. Kate met him at the door raising her mouth for a kiss. They went inside.

"Would you like some wine?" Kate asked, sitting on the sofa and watching while the dogs greeted him.

"No, thanks," Bob answered, still standing and absently playing with the dogs. "Wine's really not what I had in mind."

"Coffee?" Kate felt the same tension in him that she'd noticed that afternoon.

"Nope." His reply was almost curt.

"Is there anything you *do* want?" There was a trace of impatience in her tone.

Bob just gazed at her silently, a long level look filled with meaning. Kate got the message. She felt the message traveling through her body like a current of electricity, tingling all the way down to her toes.

"Oh, ho . . . Anticipation?" She smiled up at him.

"How about the end of anticipation?" He pulled her up from the sofa and gathered her up into his arms, enfolding her in a warm hug.

"So this is not a seduction, huh? No kissing me until I can't resist? You're not going to sweep me away on a tide of passion? You want me to make a conscious choice?" She smiled at him, then reached for his hand and the simple touch of their hands was electric. "I just hope none of the little darlings wake up," she said, as she started towards the stairs.

"They never have when I've been over, but we can wait if you want." Bob halted their progress.

"Bob, it'll be another fifteen years before the twins are eighteen, and I hate to wait. We'd better just go for it now." Kate began to pull on his arm and made a great show of dragging him up the stairs.

Of course, she didn't mention that in two days, all three of her children were going with her mother to visit her grandmother for a couple of weeks and she would have the house all to herself.

She hadn't told Bob for two reasons: first, she didn't want to seem like she was getting rid of the children just so that they could be alone; and second, she didn't want him to delay this moment because of the children. She was concerned about them too, but she was not about to let him get practical and deny their passion, she wanted him too much for that.

"Thank goodness!" Bob said as they got to her bedroom. "Somehow tonight seems like the right time to me. I feel like I'm about to explode if I don't make love to you. I can't wait a moment longer. I'm just not used to the idea of making love with your kids in the next room."

"Believe me, it's new to me too." She brought her mouth up to his for a soft, tender kiss. "But I don't want to wait either, not for anything. I want you too much."

They both paused for a moment, feeling nervous in spite of their passion. They stood there, beside her bed, motionless for an eternal moment.

"I can't believe I feel so shy suddenly," Kate smiled and continued softly, "when I want you so much."

"Me too, is it anticipation?" He stroked her long hair gently.

"Too much anticipation, and not enough action." Kate reached for his face. "It's been such a long time for me. It seems like a lifetime." She searched his eyes, "Bob, just so you know, there was only Joe before, and remember how shy I am. I want you but I'm so self-conscious about my body especially after three babies that if I seem shy, please don't think it's hesitation or second thoughts."

"We'll take it easy, love." He kissed her gently. "There's no need to rush and, Kate, there's no need for you to feel self-conscious about your body. For one thing, I've already seen it, remember? And, in spite of how we met, it really isn't just your looks that I care about. It's the real you, the woman who can carry on with her life after such a devastating loss, and make a good life for herself and her kids. Face it, Kate, you are intelligent, strong, brave, funny, kind, and very, very, sexy." The words were each punctuated with a kiss.

65

"And I'm still shy," she kissed him back, "but we can fix that."

They stood there, kissing softly just inside her bedroom door. In spite of their hunger for each other, there was no need to rush now that the decision was made. They savored each other's kisses, tongues meeting in a loving duel.

At first they were hardly touching except for their mouths, and her hands cupping his face. His hands went around her waist and began slowly sliding up and down her back, finally coming to rest, cuddling her bottom. He pulled her tightly against him for a moment so that she felt the proof of his desire, then he moved slightly back and slid his hands between their bodies. Without breaking off the kiss, he began to unbutton her blue, silk blouse then gently eased it off her shoulders. Her breath was coming in quick little gasps. For once she had worn a bra, something she usually discarded as soon as she got off work.

It was so unusual for her that Bob couldn't resist asking her, "Why did you wear a bra tonight?"

She smiled a smile that was as old as the caves. "So you could take it off me."

"You planned this?" He was astonished.

"Me? Of course not. I was just going to wait, modestly and patiently, like the lady I am, for you to suggest it. I'd never bring it up." She turned and pulled down the colorful quilted bedspread, and the crisp white sheets.

"Sweetheart, you brought it up the first time we met." Bob gave her a lecherous leer, then grinned and reached out to unfasten her lacy, mauve bra with exquisite slowness, his hands staying to cup her breasts from behind as he whispered in her ear, "And I saw you looking, so you had to know."

Discarding the bra, he turned her around and bent his head to take first one and then the other breast into his mouth. He was gently sucking and licking them until both her nipples stood out. She pulled his polo shirt over his head then trailed her own set of kisses down his muscled chest, pausing to lick his nipples.

"Where's the shyness I thought I would have to ease you through?"

She whispered, in a breathless tone, "It seems to have disappeared on its own. Isn't that amazing?"

"It means that we're right together." He whispered, "This is meant to be."

He slid her shorts down her long, smooth legs almost causing her knees to buckle and fail to support her. She stepped back, and sat shakily on the edge of the bed, and reached for his belt.

In a timeless moment, his eyes widened and his breath seemed to catch in his throat. She slowly unbuckled his belt and then undid the top button and slowly, carefully eased down the zipper of his jeans. She pushed his jeans down to the floor and he stepped out of them, pausing just long enough to get rid of his tennis shoes and socks.

He lovingly took her hands, pulled her up, and slowly, tenderly eased her dainty lace underwear down her legs. She returned the favor ridding him of his plain white jockey shorts, carefully easing them over his arousal. He lifted her out of the tangle around her feet, and laid her on the bed.

He laid down beside her, looking at her, filled with wonder at the many women she was. A hot combination of shy girl and bold woman, of delicate refined lady and fiery vixen, of tender mother and passionate lover.

He reached out and took her into his arms, showering kisses all over her face and hair then finally claiming her mouth in a searing, passionate kiss. His hands roamed all over her body, down past the fullness of her breasts to the curve of her stomach. Slowly, tantalizingly he slid one hand lower still, past her waist, down until he came to her soft curls. He began to make love to her with his hand, gently stroking the center of her femininity. His mouth left hers, and went exploring, searching out a delicate ear, and nibbling at her succulent neck.

All the time he murmured soft love words, between the kisses and nibbles, praising her body and telling her how wonderful she was. She arched her back and closed her eyes, letting all the sensations wash over her and drinking in his words. Her hands slipped down to his manhood and she lovingly began to stroke him. Suddenly they both froze as they heard a small voice cry out.

"Mommy!"

She held her breath for just a second then called out, "I'm coming Sarah, just a minute. God, I'm sorry, Love. I'll be right back," she said, giving him a light kiss and quickly pulling a nightgown over her head.

Kate went in to find out what her daughter needed. She found the little girl crying from a bad dream, so she sat on the side of the bed and talked to her. She gave her a sip of water and calmed her fears and held her until Sarah went back to sleep. Kate kissed Sarah's forehead and then went back to her bedroom.

"How is she?" Bob asked, with gentle concern.

"Sarah's fine, it was just a bad dream. I hope it wasn't too much of a mood killer." She winked at him as she slowly pulled the nightgown up over her head.

Her actions were simple and uncalculated, but the effect she achieved was as sensual as any movements of the most expert exotic dancer.

"Sweetheart, an atom bomb couldn't kill my mood right now." Smiling slowly and lovingly he asked, "How about you?"

"All I know is that I want you so badly, I almost wanted to strangle the poor little dear." Kate got back into the bed. "Coming?"

"I will be, soon." He grinned and moved over beside her. "So, where were we?"

She flipped her hair back over her shoulder and lowered her mouth down almost to his manhood. She whispered, "Right about here," before taking him into her mouth in an intimate kiss.

His hands tangled in her hair. He laid back and let the sensations flow through every fiber of his being for a long, luscious moment.

Finally, he pulled her up to kiss her mouth. "I love this, I especially love having you do this but I want to be inside you." He rolled her over onto her back and stretched out on top of her, gazing at her raptly.

"I love you," he whispered as he entered her, sliding into her warmth and wetness, filling her completely. "We fit together beautifully don't we, love?" he murmured in her ear as he began to move inside her.

She gave herself over to the sensations that were flooding her senses, murmuring incoherent love words into his ear. She met the motions of his body thrust for thrust, her rhythms and passion matching his perfectly. It was magical, there was none of the awkwardness lovers can have when it's their first time together, nothing tentative or held back.

She was past rational thinking, moving quickly towards her climax. All speech was beyond her now; she was only capable of little gurgling sounds in the back of her throat. Together they reached a peak of pleasure that left them both breathless and shivering.

She was breathing heavily, recovering from the pleasurable exertion, when she finally found her voice. "Bob, this is so incredible. Have I told you that I love you, too?" She pulled him to her for a tender kiss.

"No, but I hoped you did. I knew what we had was more than attraction. You're not the kind of woman to go to bed with someone for plain old-fashioned lust or we'd have found a way to do it the first day we met. Instead, we waited forever." Bob gently stroked her hair off her damp forehead.

"It was more like a week and a half," she protested, teasing.

"It seemed like forever to me. How did we ever get so lucky?" He kissed her hair.

"We both have a dear friend who is a world champion matchmaker." She kissed him.

"I still say I owe her a raise," he agreed, nibbling on her neck.

"No, I'll just offer babysitting services for her sometime after her baby is born," she mumbled dreamily

"Baby?" He was surprised. A second later the word seemed to register with him and his head shot up. "Oh no!"

"She hasn't told you yet?" Kate was puzzled at his expression.

"That's not it. Forget Laura. I mean, her news is great, but when you said the word 'baby' it reminded me of something. I just remembered that we forgot to use any protection." Bob looked guilty.

"Oh boy, some responsible adults we are." She counted in her head, "I should be okay, as far as pregnancy, and I've been tested, I'm healthy."

"Me too." He looked a little embarrassed. "The thing is, I came prepared. I have protection in my pocket where it does no good at all."

"I stopped and bought some, today, just in case you forgot." She laughed ruefully, "They're in the bathroom, also doing us no good at all."

"Kate, how did you know it was going to be tonight?" Bob asked softly.

"I could feel the tension, the waiting in you at work today, and knew I was feeling same. I knew you were as tense as a coiled spring, like I was, and you had the same need for it to be released." Kate kissed his chest.

"Well, at least some of the sexual tension was released," Bob stroked her hair, reveling in the touch of her mouth on his nipples, "but that's not all I want from you. There's more to my feelings than sexual tension, and you know it."

"Mine, too," she muttered, her mouth busy trailing slowly down his chest.

"As far as the sexual release, though, it was pretty darn spectacular," Bob pulled her up for a kiss, "definitely worth another try."

"Well let's see, first, Sarah interrupted us and next, we forgot to use protection. If we can be spectacular together with all that going on, what else can go wrong?" Kate was more bemused than anything else.

"I could tell you that twins run in my family, too." Bob planted a quick kiss on her smooth shoulder.

"Great." She sighed dramatically, "Well, we'll just hope for the best and remember to be more responsible next time."

"When is the next time going to be?" he asked expectantly.

She reached over and grabbed his jeans off the floor and threw them at him. "If you dig into your pocket, *now*, would be good."

"I was hoping you'd say that." He got the necessary item out of his pocket and put it to use, then reached for her. "Works for me."

The minute he touched her, the magic began again. This time, like the first time, they found their rhythms were perfectly matched. Feelings of love and tenderness merged magically with fire and passion, and once again they were transported towards an explosion of pleasure.

They cuddled in the afterglow, talking about themselves. Kate told him more about her plans and dreams, and how empty her life had been from the time she'd been widowed. Bob discussed his desire to get out of Southern California and into a more rural area where he could have several acres of land. He wanted horses and a swimming pool, and lots of room to raise a family.

"And dogs, of course," she added in a matter-of-fact tone.

"Love you, love your dogs, is that it?" He kissed her. "Of course, dogs."

She found out that he was ticklish and he learned that she

loved to have her back scratched. She discovered that running her foot down the length of his leg had an instant effect on his libido. He realized that she had a special, sensitive place, between her breasts that drove her to frenzy. They both knew that there was still plenty to be explored and discovered. Finally and very reluctantly, Bob decided that he'd better leave.

She lay on the bed watching him get dressed. It was like covering up a beautiful statue and she told him so; to her surprise he blushed, just the faintest shade of pink, but it was there.

"Bob, I hate to bring this up," Kate said, "but I'm really nervous about tomorrow. I hate the idea of being thought of as a thief by my friends at work. "

"Don't worry, Kate, you know we're in this together." He leaned over to kiss her tenderly.

"I know, and I trust you." She pulled him down for another kiss. "I don't want you to leave."

"I have to, there's a lot of work to do tomorrow and there are your kids to think of," he said reluctantly.

"You're right, but I don't like it," she pouted, and then reached up and pulled him down for a kiss.

"If you keep kissing me like that you make it hard for me to go," Bob admitted.

"I'd like to make it damn well impossible." Her expression looked like a cat that had gotten into the cream.

Just before he left, he sobered for a minute, "Kate, if anything happens, please, no abortion?"

"I'm not the type. If anything happens, it happens," she replied. "But, if twins run in my family and in yours, that means we might have quadruplets." She laughed so hard she almost fell off the bed at his facial expression.

"That's not how it works!" he protested, then he looked at her full of a man's uncertainty. "Is it?"

"Had you going for a minute there, big guy, didn't I?" Kate laughed and threw a pillow at him. He leaned over kissed her again, then left.

The next morning she called Laura at home very early, long before work. "Hey, do me a favor? If Bob asks you any weird questions about how when twins run on both the mother's and father's sides of the family it might mean quadruplets, say yes."

"Does this mean you've been doing something I should know about?" Laura sat up in bed, instantly alert, but the line was already dead.

Chapter Six

The next morning Kate was an hour late getting up for work. Somebody sneaky had turned off her alarm clock. She lay there in bed, stretching and feeling languid and luxuriant. She was very conscious of the tiny aches and pains from muscles that had been unused for so long. She knew she had to get up and get moving fast, but she couldn't seem to do it. She sighed; she would be late for work again for the second day in a row.

It wasn't part of her reckless, irresponsible employee act, and since her mom now came over to baby sit, it wasn't getting the kids dressed and ready to go. This time the reason for her tardiness was simple, she just couldn't work up the energy to get out of bed.

She felt wonderful but her enthusiasm and energy was sadly lacking. She managed to call to Laura from the bed, but the idea of getting up and feeding the kids seemed like an insurmountable chore. Finally, she forced herself to get up and into the shower, hoping it would help.

Luckily her mother was downstairs already feeding the kids by the time she made it to the kitchen. She did have an awkward moment when her mother took a good long look at her. She was so relaxed, peaceful and curiously content that she couldn't hide a small, wistful smile and her mother was instantly suspicious.

"Is that what you're wearing to the office?" she asked in a slightly disapproving tone.

Kate had on her yellow sundress, but she had replaced the insert at the neck, and put a crisp white blazer over it. It was only moderately successful, but for some reason she wanted to wear Bob's favorite dress to work that day.

"Yes, Mom. It's a fairly casual office and I just wanted to wear it today." She poured herself some orange juice. "May I say you look very nice today?"

Her mother did indeed look good, cool and comfortable in crisp tan linen slacks and a melon colored camp shirt. At fifty, she was trim and neat, with very few signs of age except for laugh lines at the corners of her mouth. Her dark auburn hair was shoulder length and carefully styled. All in all, she was still a vital, attractive woman, a fact that Kate's father was extremely happy about.

"Of course you may say I look nice today, even if it's just an excuse to change the subject. You, however, look tired. Are you working too hard dear? Eating right? Getting to bed on time?" Her mother questioned her closely.

She couldn't help herself, at her mother's last question Kate flushed. "Mom! I'm okay. If there's something bothering me it's just, um, the strain of getting used to a new job."

"Kate, you never could lie to me," her mother said sternly. Then her voice softened, "If I had to take a guess, I'd say you've finally found a man. A good sexy man, judging by the glow on your face. You've had a romantic evening, haven't you? No wonder you're so lazy today. Didn't you remember that today is a work day?"

Kate's slight flush became a full-blown blush. "Please, Mom."

She felt like a teenager again. Her mom had lectured her the same way when she stayed out too late on a school night. She looked over at her kids, but they weren't paying any attention to the adults' conversation. In fact, they were sneaking food to the dogs.

"Suzy! Sarah! Sam! Eat your food." She got up and put the dogs outside, fastening the doggie door shut behind them. "The dogs have food of their own."

"So tell me about him and I'll get off your back," her mother prodded gently.

"Okay." Kate gave up all pretenses. "He's my new boss, and he is so sexy and gorgeous it's hard not to swoon at the sight of him. And he's got the, um, forget that part, Mom. But he's not just a pretty package, he's also a great guy." Kate's eyes glazed over as she described Bob to her mother.

"It's usually a bad idea to get involved with your boss." The voice of maternal reason.

"I know. But it would be total insanity to pass up a man like this and my mom didn't raise any crazy daughters." Kate grinned, "Besides, it's too late, I have no choice in the matter. Let's be serious here, I'm a goner, Mom."

"Is this just a romance or could this lead to marriage?" Her mom hugged her closely.

"Truthfully, mom?" She considered the idea. "It's way too soon to be sure, but I'd be surprised if it didn't end in marriage," Kate grabbed her car keys, "if I don't get fired for being late to work."

"So go. What's holding you up?" She gave her daughter a push out the door.

"Keep a close watch on Teddy today, Mom. Her temperature was down a little last night. Will you watch it for me today?" Kate stopped at the door. "I'll call you from the office to check on her and go over last minute details for your trip to Grandma's with the kids, okay?"

"I'll watch her, but remember, if she seems to be doing okay around noon, I'm going to leave early. I've arranged to have my friend, Martha, come over so that I can run some errands. I have so many things to do in order to get ready that I think I'm going to go nuts. Martha will play with the kids until you get home and she can also keep an eye on Teddy for you. Okay? I have the vet's phone number right next to your work number. Don't worry." She hugged her daughter. "Have a good day."

When Kate arrived at the office, she barely got past her

curious co-workers and to her desk before her phone rang. She sat at her desk and answered it.

Laura was on the line. "Kate, get in my office, now!"

Kate just started to stand up when her phone rang again.

This time it was Bob. "Kate, my office, now!"

Kate hurried into Laura's office. "What did you two do, work out a script? Bob called me after you did. He wants me in his office, too."

"I'll let you go to him, then. I just wanted to find out what that early morning phone call was all about." Laura questioned, "I mean, have you got any reason to worry about having quadruplets? Twins? Even one? There are a few steps in that process, you know."

"Really?" Kate acted incredulously. "Tell me about it."

"Somehow I think it's too late." She laughed. "Sarah, Suzy and Sam are evidence that you already know how to make babies. So get going, but come back when we can talk. And yes, I did notice you're wearing your sexy yellow sundress."

Kate grinned at her, "This old thing?"

She hurried to Bob's office. She walked in and shut the door behind her. She looked at him, noting the slight signs of fatigue, the tired eyes and lack of energy in his movements, the stifled yawn. She was secretly pleased that Bob seemed to be worn out too.

"What took you so long?" He yelled loud enough to be heard all throughout the office area.

He took her in his arms and sank to the leather sofa, pulling her down on top of himself in a passionate embrace.

She pulled back just enough to answer, "Laura paged me first."

"What did she want?" He kissed her and stroked her hair.

"She had dual purposes, the brat." Kate nuzzled his neck. "She wanted to make it look like I was being called on the carpet for being late, and she wanted to ask me, ah, some personal questions."

"About me?" he asked. "About us?"

"Why would we talk about you?" she answered, being evasive. "A little conceited today, are we?"

"Come on, what questions?" Bob persisted, somehow sensing that he was the subject of this mysterious conversation.

"Girl talk, about babies," Kate said firmly. "Personal stuff."

"Does she know that we made love?" He decided to use kisses to persuade her to spill the required information.

"Well, I never actually told her." Kate smiled at him, matching his kisses with her own. "I did not say the words, 'Bob and I made fantastic love over and over last night,' but the CIA could use her for interrogating spies."

Kate paused for another delicious kiss. "Except for figuring out who the thief is, she's got a real blind spot there."

"But why were you late today?" Bob teased, "Didn't you get enough sleep last night?"

"Funny thing, that's just what Mom asked me when she came over to watch the kids. She didn't know that some wonderful," she kissed him, "devious, sexy person turned off my alarm clock. By the way, you look a little worn out, too. Are you sure you weren't up too long last night?"

"Are you very sure you don't want to rethink the way you phrased that question?" he teased, watching the flush spread over her face. "I thought I was, um, up just long enough."

"And so you were. But back to my mother, she thinks I'm having an office romance," Kate laughed.

"Did you tell her about us?" he asked softly.

"I tried not to. I wanted to keep it to ourselves, just to savor the feelings, for a little while. Do you know what I mean?" She looked up at him, Bob nodded. "But heck, she's my mom. She read between the blushes."

"What did she think?" he asked, interested in the dynamics of this mother-daughter relationship.

"I think she's thrilled, but she's also going to reserve final approval until she checks you out. After all, she's never heard a word about you before today. My dad will be the one to give you a really hard time." She pulled away from him and stood up. "They haven't met you yet, remember."

"Are you ready to go into action?" he asked. At her reluctant nod he kissed her and then raised his voice, "Well Missy, a thousand dollars is a lot of money to be short, and it's in your area. It had better turn up soon. Remember I've got my eyes on you!" Then his voice dropped, sexy and low, "And my mouth, and my hands and my . . ." He punctuated each phrase with a kiss, then raised his voice again. "Now get back to work and this better not happen again!"

"We'd both be disappointed if it didn't," she said as she stood up and walked over to the door. At the door she turned and looked back over her shoulder and smiled at him. Then she left his office trying to look angry and defiant.

"What a jerk!" she fumed as she stormed across the office. "As if I'd ever . . ." She looked around and quickly stopped talking.

Instantly Cheryl put an arm around Kate's shoulders. "How do they ever expect you to get anything done? All they ever do is yell at you," she said with concern in her big brown eyes. "Both of them."

Rita came over. "What's up?"

Cheryl answered, "Laura and Bob both have had her on the carpet already, and it's only nine-thirty."

"You poor kid." Rita enfolded her in her ample arms. "I just don't understand it. Bob and Laura used to be so nice. They never lost their tempers with anyone else. I mean, you may have been late a couple of times, but you've really done a good job on catching up on the backlog in Accounts Payable."

Mary stated angrily, "I'm going to go in and talk to Laura. Even if they do have a legitimate reason to complain about your tardiness only one of them should lecture you about it. You don't deserve to be given two tongue-lashings."

She stormed off, a petite dynamo, looking like she was ready to storm hell with a glass of water.

Kate kept her face buried in Rita's arms to keep herself from laughing out loud. She remembered all too well exactly how it felt when Bob gave her a tongue-lashing, and she'd take one from him anytime she could.

A short time later Laura entered her cubicle. "We have to talk. Let's go to my office."

The two friends went to Laura's office.

"Whew!" Laura sat down. "I really got yelled at. Remind me never to underestimate Mary. She told me that the gang thinks Bob and I are too hard on you and it had better stop if we want to have anyone working for us. Only she used a lot of real interesting words to get her point across. I can't believe she talked to her boss like that."

"I never realized that it might be as hard on you as it will be for me. At least I get sympathy, you get to be an ogre, and you're getting so good at it." Kate laughed as Laura stuck her tongue out at her. "I hope you don't wind up with a revolution on your hands. Maybe I'll try to smooth their ruffled feathers."

"It wouldn't work, and it might blow your cover. I'd better warn Bob he's going to be getting dirty looks all day," Laura said. "Hell! Mary may even chew his cute tush all the way off."

"Go protect him, I can't love a man with no tush!" She laughingly shoved Laura towards the door.

Laura looked back at Kate, her eyes wide. "Love? Are you admitting you're in love? You did spend the night together? Come on, tell all."

"Interrogate me later; go rescue my man from the revolt of the aggravated accounting staff," Kate laughed.

"Sounds like a B movie," Laura quipped. "The kind of thing where the controller and his beautiful assistant are both in danger of being found hacked to death, with a hatchet sticking out from one of their bodies."

"Yeah, and the heroine is going to mangle the assistant controller if the assistant controller doesn't go protect the controller," Kate told her sternly.

"I thought the assistant controller was the heroine," Laura muttered as she left the office. After a couple of steps she turned back and said, "Hey Kate, remember, it's *my* office, don't you have some work to do in yours?"

Kate returned to her cubicle and spent the morning working to keep up on the Accounts Payable paperwork. It was a tedious day. She finally input her data and ran a summary of which invoices were ready for payment. Shortly before lunch, a man she had never met before brought a large, bulky envelope and placed it on her desk.

"Hi! I'm Frank." His smile was warm.

Kate finished inputting a sum before she looked up. She saw a handsome man in his mid-twenties. He was tall and had blonde hair, brown eyes, and a super, friendly smile.

"That's good, frankness is an important quality in a man," she told him in a cool, noncommittal voice. "But who are you?"

Frank looked at her, puzzled for a second, then he laughed. "No, Frank's my name."

"So you're not especially frank?" she asked, laughing.

"No, actually I'm more earnest," he said sincerely. "It's very important to be earnest."

"You have a real identity crisis there, Ernie." She smiled and held out a hand, "I'm Kate."

"Kate, dainty Kate, the sweetest Kate in all of . . ." He kissed her hand.

"Cool it, Petruchio. This shrew doesn't need taming." She looked at the envelope. "What's this?"

"These are the bimonthly reports from the retail stores. You get a copy just so you can match any products against invoices, since some of our purchases are drop shipped to the stores," he explained.

"More work, gee, thanks a lot." She smiled at him. "So what else is new around here?"

"Not much, you're the newest thing around." He sat on the edge of her desk.

"Maybe so, but I'll bet you're the freshest thing around." She stood up and started to hustle him out of her cubicle, but he stopped at the entrance and asked her out to lunch.

"Who's asking me? Frank or Ernie?" she asked mischievously.

"The invitation's from Frank. Ernie's still loading sixteen tons, and Who's on first," he laughed.

She thought for a moment. It would be a good chance to find out if he knew anything about the thefts. "I need another half-hour to finish running this report, okay?"

"Sure, I'll be back." He left, whistling softly.

Shortly after that, her phone rang. It was Bob. "Kate, I know it's not wise but meet me for lunch, please."

"Gee, sorry Bob, I already have a hot lunch date." She paused dramatically. "Frank asked me to go out to lunch with him." There was dead silence on the intercom.

"And you'd rather go out with him?" Bob suddenly appeared in the opening to her cubicle, his voice was ominously low.

"No, of course not, it's part of my investigation. A new path to follow, so to speak." Her voice was also low to avoid being overheard. "You sound jealous, and you know you shouldn't be, even if he is nice, handsome and single."

"He's handsome?" The tone was ominously low.

"Hey, boss, take it easy," Kate smiled at the jealously implied in his tone. "It's a working lunch."

"Just don't enjoy it too much, and remember I get to take you to dinner." This was definitely an order.

"And after dinner? Boss, sir?" she answered with exaggerated meekness. "Who's going to take me then?"

"I'll take you then, too," he answered boldly.

"Take me where?" she asked, trying to sound confused.

He glanced around, then replied, "To bed, where I'll make love to you all night long."

"Good plan. I'm glad you thought of it." She pushed him out of the cubicle. "Now let me get some work done today because I have a feeling I'll be rather tired again tomorrow morning, and so will you."

As Kate left for her lunch date with Frank, she spotted Bob leaving the building with the most beautiful woman she'd ever seen. She had long, raven black hair, a slender, perfect figure, and an arresting face.

She asked Frank, "Who's that with Bob?"

"I don't know, maybe it's his new girlfriend. He seems suspiciously happy lately. She's really gorgeous, isn't she?" Frank grinned at her.

"If you like the type," she said, then paused and laughed at herself. "Meow! You'd better get me a saucer of milk for lunch."

"Come on, little cat. Maybe I'll even get you a nice fresh mouse." He turned and looked at her, his gaze full of speculation. "Maybe I shouldn't say this but you sounded jealous just then."

"Me? Jealous of Bob? I've just met him, don't be ridiculous." Kate tried to sound indignant but she blushed. "Besides, he just spent the whole morning yelling at me."

"Either you're in love with the guy and jealous as heck *and* lying about it, or you just got sunburned in world record time," Frank kidded her, as he held the car door for her.

"Just wait till you fall in love," she muttered as she got into the car. "Scratch that, Frank. It's a secret, please."

"Why are the good women already taken?" Frank asked in an exaggerated, plaintive voice as he walked around the car to his door.

"Because we *are* good women, you silly man," Kate told him

archly.

He opened the car door and got in. "But what's the problem with you and Bob? Why are you both hiding the fact that you're in love? And why is he always yelling at you? Everyone in the office is talking about it."

"The yelling part is easy, he yells at me so that we can keep people from finding out that we're involved with each other, outside of work. It also gives me an excuse to spend some time behind his office door." She paused, trying to think of a good explanation for hiding her relationship with Bob. "We're keeping our relationship a secret because it would cause friction with my co-workers. No matter what we did, they'd think Bob was somehow playing favorites."

Kate knew it was a weak reason to hide her relationship with Bob. She thought for a moment and decided to tell Frank part of the truth. It was a risk she felt justified in taking. She instinctively trusted Frank.

"There's been some money stolen from the company and I'm the logical suspect. I didn't take it Frank, I swear, but if it looks like Bob and I are too close . . ." she trailed off, trying to find the words.

"Somebody might think that either he's not investigating you as vigorously as he should, or that you're using your feminine wiles on him," Frank finished the thought.

"Right. And there's nothing calculated in our relationship, we just fell in love. It was practically love at first sight." Kate hesitated and then added, "I know that Bob's a decent, honest man. There's no way, even loving me, that he would let me steal from the company."

"Your act is flawed though. There's talk all over the office about how Bob's treating you. It's not like either Bob or Laura to yell at a temp." Frank pointed out, "If your work wasn't up to par, he'd just replace you."

"Maybe we'll have to polish our act if I'm there long enough to worry about it." She gazed at Frank, a long, steady gaze.

They arrived at the restaurant, were seated, and placed their orders.

"So let's drop it for now, Romeo, and have lunch," Kate said as a waiter appeared with their lunches.

"The name is Petruchio, remember?" he teased.

"I can't wait until a shrew finds you and tames you," she replied as she cut up her grilled chicken breast. "When it happens, I hope I get ringside seats. Maybe I'll sic Laura on you."

He made a cross using his two forefingers, and backed away from Kate feigning fright. "No, not that! Please spare me. I'm a good guy!"

"When Laura and I get through with you, you'll be even better. Just don't worry about a thing." She grinned wickedly, then reached out to pat the back of his hand. "Somewhere out there is a good, stubborn, spitfire of a woman just waiting for you and maybe we'll help you find her. She'll drive you crazy before you even know what's happening."

"Please Kate," Frank pleaded, "don't be so helpful."

Over lunch Kate learned that Frank, among his other jobs, acted as a courier for the company's money on rare occasions. She liked him a lot and felt an instant kinship with his quirky sense of humor, but she couldn't help wondering why he wasn't listed as a suspect. Almost hating herself for the thought, she decided to ask Laura about him that afternoon.

As they drove back to the office, she had a favor to ask Frank. "Please, help us keep our secret. I hope I can trust you."

"Of course I'll keep your secret." Frank quoted, "*I have a feeling this is the start of a beautiful friendship.*" Frank smiled as he quoted. "You know, I'm not stupid though, I do realize what you told me is not the whole story. You're not really a suspect; you're the one investigating the thefts."

"How did you know?" she asked quickly.

"I don't think Bob realizes I know this, but I know that money's been missing long before you came to work. I'm fairly sure that no one else knows about it, or I would have heard rumors. I just realized that there's no logical reason we should have to replace the Accounts Payable clerk every two months. Something had to be wrong." Frank looked sideways at her. "If I can help in any way, let me know."

"I sure will. Frank, I'll have to tell Bob that you know, okay?" She glanced at him.

"Of course, if I wanted you to keep something a secret from Bob, it would have to be something juicier than that," he laughed. "Now if we went to a hotel and made mad, passionate love, that's a secret I'd keep."

"Dream on, lover boy," Kate laughed, shaking her head.

After lunch Kate walked into Laura's office and asked Laura her opinion about Frank.

"Frank?" Laura replied to Kate's question. "He takes locked bags of money between the stores and this office occasionally but he doesn't have the key." Laura thought out loud, "He could have found another way to embezzle but I don't think so. For one thing, he's on a fast track to promotion."

"You'd hate to think any of the others are the thief either, wouldn't you?" Kate prompted.

"That's what's so hard about this," Laura said sadly. "I like everyone. I even trust everyone."

"I'm sure Frank's innocent, too. But I'm going to look over everyone I can think of, not just the women in the office," Kate stated.

"We looked at others too, but go ahead. I hope you can clear all of us." She sighed, "You do realize that Bob and I are under suspicion, too."

"Some detective I'd make, I never thought of either of you." Kate worried, "Is someone making things hard on you?"

"Well, the division head, Mr. Watson, hasn't been too bad.

But corporate, um, corporate wants this solved or they want both of our heads on a platter. Soon."

"So, as they say, time is of the essence." Kate started to leave. "By the way, who was the woman Bob went out to lunch with?"

"Sorry, Kate, I don't know." Laura was no help at all.

Kate went into her cubicle and got Bob on the phone. "Are you alone?"

"Yes, what's up?" he asked.

"Pull your angry boss act and summon me again. I want to talk," she replied.

A short time later Bob stuck his head in and briskly said, "Kate, please come into my office, again!"

She pulled the door shut behind her. "Tell me Bob, who was your lunch date?"

Bob laughed until his sides hurt. "So that's what you wanted to talk about. That was a business lunch. Elissa's going to be a model in our new brochure. She's very beautiful, but she's also very dull. No spark, and very few brains."

"Bob, really, that sounds so chauvinistic. Not all beautiful women are dumb." Kate protested, "Lots of models have plenty of brains."

"I agree, after all you're a beautiful woman and you're extremely intelligent," he said smoothly.

"Good save." She laughed.

"I have met lots of intelligent models, but she's not one of them. She's like a pretty picture. She's great to look at but hard to talk to. Her subject matter is limited to two things: the latest styles and her looks. If she really gets going, she might even talk about how she looks in the latest styles. She could put me into a coma. Let's face it, she just wasn't you." He pulled her down onto his lap and began to nuzzle her neck.

"That's funny, my lunch date was very charming, handsome, funny and witty . . ." She paused, savoring the feel of his warm mouth on her soft neck. "And he still wasn't you. I do have something to report though, and I hope I did the right thing."

She told Bob what she had said to Frank and also Frank's guess about the truth of the situation.

"I hope I didn't mess things up," she finished.

"I had eliminated Frank as a suspect in my own investigation. I just didn't tell you because I wanted you to look at everybody with fresh eyes." He kissed her gently. "So let's forget all about him and talk about us."

Their lips met in a lingering kiss, then Kate sighed. "Did I mention that my kids were going out of town?"

"No, you didn't mention it. Where are they going and when?" he asked between kisses.

"My mom's taking them to her mother's ranch for a week or two. They're leaving tomorrow," she told him.

"Why are they leaving tomorrow? Won't they be gone when Teddy has her puppies?" He was puzzled. "That seems strange."

"The trip was planned long before Teddy got pregnant. I almost changed the plans, but I thought the new mom could use a moment's peace," Kate explained, "and the puppies could grow just a little bit stronger."

"Hey! I just thought of something. If you and I were both so nervous about making love with the kids in the next room, why didn't you tell me that the kids were leaving this weekend?" he questioned. "We could have waited one more night."

"Did you want to wait any longer?" she asked him gently. "I sure didn't. And I don't regret making love to you last night."

"No I didn't want to wait another second to love you, but I would have, if you had asked," he told her quietly.

"That's why I didn't ask." She kissed him gently on his forehead. "I'd better go back to work. I'll tell them that you were annoyed at me but eventually apologized. Maybe it will throw them off balance and help save your reputation as a fair employer."

"You throw me off balance," he admitted.

"Hey boss, you'd better not flirt with me like that, I'm the hired help." She opened the door and left.

As soon as she stepped out of Bob's office the other women came over to her. Mary asked, "Was he mad at you again?"

"He was a little annoyed at first, but I explained what was going on and he apologized," Kate replied with a smile. "He was really very decent about it."

She went into her cubicle and went back to work leaving her co-workers staring after her.

Kate spent the afternoon working on the cash trail, matching cash register tapes and cash room reports. She began to see a pattern, confusing and blurry, but a pattern. She placed a call to Shelly and they worked on a plan to find some answers. Shortly before she finished her work for the day, she noticed something strange about certain invoices. The ones in question had purchase orders which had been written by Laura and initialed by Bob, and the receiving slips showed that the purchases had been drop shipped to another location. She made copies of all the suspicious paperwork. She also asked Bob to provide her with a list of all the known thefts. She put everything in a briefcase so she could take them home.

Before she left, Kate told Bob that she wouldn't be in the next day. She had three major lines of investigation to pursue: the store cashiers, the cash room clerks, and the trail from purchasing to payables. It looked like there was more than one thief, and they seemed to be unconnected. The major thief, the embezzler, seemed to be one of three people: Laura, Bob, or the purchasing manager, Jerry Weisner. She also had two paths to follow: the cash receipts and the paper trail. Finally she had something she could really dig into and investigate. She could hardly wait to get and home begin her work.

Chapter Seven

Kate's plans changed as soon as she got home. Teddy was in labor. Martha, her mother's friend, was trying to keep the kids calm but it was obvious there was something wrong with the little dog and they were worried. Martha wasn't able to calm the kids down, she was fidgeting and fretting as much as they were.

"I'm so glad you're finally home, Kate." The agitated woman paced. "She seemed fine but about fifteen minutes ago she started acting sick. I called your office but you were already gone."

"She's fine, Martha," Kate reassured her. "You did a wonderful job of looking after her and the kids."

Kate sent Martha home, with her thanks. She checked the little dog and Teddy was definitely in labor. Sometimes Bostons have a hard time delivering their puppies, so just to be safe, Kate took care of a few special errands.

First, she called Ida and had her come over to sit with Teddy who was fussing too much to get into her whelping box. Then she put Charger outside. Finally, she changed clothes, poured herself a cold soda and called Bob. She told him not to come over.

"I'll probably wind up spending the night at the pet clinic." She sounded both disappointed and excited. "Teddy might need a C-section."

"Would you like me to come too?" Bob offered.

"I'd love for you to come, but you need your sleep."

"I'll be over as soon as I can, but I'm pretty tied up in something for a while," Bob volunteered.

Finally, she took the kids over to her parents' house. The

kids didn't know what was wrong with Teddy, so they balked at leaving the little dog. Kate bribed them with stories about the lambs, calves, and ponies at her grandmother's place.

Sam, for one, decided he liked the idea of ponies and seemed willing to go but nothing worked with the twins until she brought out the emotional big guns: kittens. Her grandmother also had a litter of kittens. Finally Suzy and Sarah agreed to go over to Grandma's.

She got them into her car as quickly as possible, mentally thanking herself that she packed for the trip two days earlier, and drove them to her parents' house.

The way her day was going it was inevitable. For the first time in weeks, she found herself face to face with her father. He sent the kids inside to watch television in a voice that stopped any protest flat. Then he turned to Kate.

"I hear you have a new boyfriend." He spoke gruffly, "What's the matter? Do you think you're too grown-up to introduce your boyfriends to your parents? Or is there something to hide?"

Kate looked up at her father; not only was he a tall, stern, dignified man, but he was standing a step higher than her on the front porch.

She shaded her eyes against the setting sun and felt the years slipping away as she told him, "Daddy, of course I'll bring him over and introduce him to you. We just haven't been seeing each other very long. There hasn't been any time yet. I want you to like him." She smiled almost timidly, "I'm sure you will."

"Is he as great as your mother told me?" His voice was still stern.

"Yes, Daddy." She hated herself for sounding so meek.

"And he's not married? Gay? Doesn't have AIDS? He's good to you in bed?" He shot the questions at her like bullets.

"No, Daddy. No, Daddy. No Daddy. Ye . . . Daddy! Darn you that's private." She flushed a deep pink but she had a wide grin.

Her dad finally relented, a wide smile broke over his face. "Well, it's about time. I'm reserving judgment until I meet him, but I'm happy for you, kid. I just hope you're using birth control."

She flushed as she thought of the first night.

"For heaven's sake! Be careful, girl. You know you're fertile as a turtle, Myrtle. I'll probably be a grandfather again in about eight months. That would be four," he reminded her.

"Or more," she regained her composure, and shot him a sideways glance, "twins run in his family, too. Good-bye Dad, give Mom my love."

She made a quick escape before he could reply.

When she got home she found out that while she was gone, Ida had gotten everything ready to take Teddy to the vet's office. She had the doggy carrier filled with soft, old pieces of blankets and a shoebox filled with several old washcloths. She waited while Kate wrote a quick note and pinned it on the front door and then helped Kate put the dog into the carrier, and the carrier into the car.

She hugged Kate, "Call me as soon as you know they're born."

"I will, thanks Ida." She returned the hug.

Bob found a note on her door when he got there; it had the clinic's name and address, and ended with the words: I love you, Kate. Bob took the note with him as he got back into the car and headed for the clinic.

He found the clinic easily, with its big bright sign: **Emergency Pet Clinic**. He parked his car and went inside. He asked about Kate and was directed into Exam Room 1. When she saw him she reached up for him, pulling him down for a quick kiss.

"How's it going?" he asked.

"The vet's examining her in the back. She might or might not need . . ." She stopped as the vet, a woman in her mid-thirties, entered.

She told them, "I think we'd better go with a c-section. We did an X-ray and it looks like a tight fit for the puppies. Bostons have such big heads for such little dogs. She has four, by the way, which is a pretty good-sized litter for her."

"Okay, let's do it," Kate answered.

"Can you help rub puppies? I can use the extra hands," the vet asked.

"Sure," Kate was glad to do it, "can you use Bob, too?"

"Of course, the more the merrier. One of the techs will get you both some masks and hats, and show you where to go." She left.

"Kate, I don't' like the sight of blood." Bob wasn't at all sure about this.

Kate laughed, "Don't worry, think of this as practice for when you become a father."

"When I become a father I plan to do it the old-fashioned way, pacing in the waiting room," he said firmly.

"Not a chance, dear." She realized what she was implying and blushed, "I mean if your wife would have anything to say about it."

"That does it then. I'm staying single." He noticed her quick frown. "Permanently."

"Don't decide yet. Wait until you see how you feel after Teddy whelps." She looked up and saw the tech. "Hey Cindy, this guy is really nervous."

"We've never lost a father yet." The young girl handed both Kate and Bob paper hats and masks, and helped the couple put them on.

Bob whispered loudly, "Does she really think I'm the father?"

"She's teasing. Teddy's a dog. Remember?" She pushed him into the small room.

She kept her eyes on the operation. Bob stayed back at first, then found himself becoming fascinated. The techs brought over the puppies, swinging them up and down to clear their nasal passages. Then they handed one each to Kate and Bob.

Cindy showed them what to do. "Rub hard, make them cry."

Both Kate and Bob worked on their little charges, while Cindy and the other tech worked on the other two. All four puppies were making little crying sounds. Fairly soon, the vet came into the room.

"Teddy is okay." She looked over each puppy in turn, checking him or her for birth defects or any other problems. "And so are these guys. By the way, three females and one male. Great markings. They're all cute as hell."

"If they're healthy, they're perfect." Kate was pleased. "Good markings are just a bonus."

"We can keep them in the incubator overnight," the vet offered, "or you can take them home now."

"I think I'll take them. I have a box for the puppies, with lots of blankets," Kate answered with a big smile. "Well, actually I'm using a shoebox and washcloths, and I have a carrier for Teddy."

"Are you sure you know the routine for caring for them at home?" the vet questioned.

"I sure do." Kate was an old hand at taking care of puppies. "This is my third litter."

"Well then, call me if you need me." The vet smiled. "I love happy nights like this. It can be very depressing." A buzzer rang, she picked up the phone, and then turned to Kate. "My good luck just ended. I've got to run, car accident."

"It's very sobering to bring a pet here at night," Kate said. "Even if your pet is okay, there are other patients here in very serious condition."

"But we have a great litter of puppies," Bob put his arm around her, "and I didn't faint."

"Think you could stand to see your own baby being born?" she teased.

"Maybe." He smiled. "It sure feels great to see and hold a

new little being."

"Or four." She flashed a sly grin at Bob. "I told you we'd have quadruplets!"

"Please God, no!" He looked at her with amused tenderness, "I *do* know that you are just pulling my leg." He picked up Teddy's carrier.

There was pure mischief in her smile. "Oh, am I?" Kate said quietly as she picked up the shoebox with the four new puppies in it. "Am I indeed?"

They took the litter home, then put Teddy and her brood in her whelping box in the den. Charger found himself banished to the kids' room without the kids or Teddy in there. He was not a happy dog. He was so curious about the puppies, making little squeaky noises in the den and he was so lonesome all by himself that he was about to burst. He was scratching at the bedroom door, trying to get out, and making little whimpering sounds. Kate and Bob both felt sorry for the little guy.

With the kids over at their grandmother's, the lovers had the house all to themselves. They turned their attention to each other, quietly but passionately making love well into the night.

Just before they drifted off to sleep Bob kissed Kate gently and said, "I can't stand it."

He got out of bed and went into the kids' room to get Charger. Kate looked at him, thinking of what a softy her new man was, to feel so sorry for a very lonesome, and very spoiled, little dog.

"Hey, my love. If you're that soft-hearted the kids are going to walk all over you," she teased as Charger curled up at their feet.

In the tender moments of just holding each other, they talked about the puppies and the kids. Kate told him about the conversation with her father.

"Daddy really wants to meet you." She grinned, "I think he's happy that I'm seeing someone, but he's going to give you a hard time just for the fun of it."

"I would if I had a daughter." Bob kissed her. "Even if she were a grown woman with kids of her own. I'll just have to find a way to make him like me."

"Oh, he'll like you even if he gives you a load of trouble. Where do you think I got my sense of humor?" she teased.

"I may be in danger here," he returned, kissing her.

"Speaking of which, I gave him the impression that I may be..." she paused, "um, in trouble."

"You mean because of the stuff going on at work?" he asked, walking right into her trap.

"No, my dear dodo. When a father thinks his daughter's in trouble that's not what he thinks of first," she said, feeling guilty.

"Your father thinks I got you pregnant?" Bob was shocked, then he gasped, "Did I? Are you?"

"How would I know? It was only yesterday that we finally made love. Remember?" She lowered her mouth to his, kissing him passionately. "The possibility exists but I doubt it. I can't be sure of course because you carelessly forgot to use protection the first time."

"I forgot?" His inflection seemed to imply differently.

"Well, okay, we forgot. Anyway, if I am you'll be the first to know," Kate yawned, "right after me."

"Did you really tell your dad all this or did he figure it out by himself," he asked, snuggling in closer and pulling her into his arms.

"He figured it out, more or less," she mumbled.

They cuddled together for a while, gently stroking and kissing each other. Then they began to talk once again. Kate told him why her mother was going to take the kids to see their great grandmother on her ranch instead of having them home playing with the puppies.

"We set the visit up before Teddy was bred and I decided not to change it. I know I'm being a mean mother, but I think it's best. My grandmother gets to see her great-grandkids, and they get to play with her kittens, along with lambs and a pony. Also it will give the puppies a little time to grow before the kids handle them. And of course, the first week or so is the time for the highest mortality rate in puppies. If something happens, which it won't, I'd rather the kids never know."

"You can't protect kids from things like that," he said firmly. "And hiding the puppies from the kids seems, well, mean."

"I'm not hiding the puppies from the kids, really, but remember just how young my kids are. They'll have a great surprise when they come home and they can enjoy the puppies just as much in two weeks. Also, I won't have to nag them constantly to leave the puppies alone, the puppies will be strong and healthy enough to play with." She continued, "I know they'll learn about mortality one day but I'd like to postpone it." She looked up at him, "Besides it gives me a little time alone."

He moved over her, "No, it doesn't."

He lowered his mouth over hers, capturing it in a kiss that took her breath away. One of his hands found the tight tangle of curls at the juncture of her thighs. "You won't be alone." His mouth moved slowly down her body until it came to the same spot his fingers had already found.

Bob left early enough Friday morning to change before work. He insisted that Kate take the day off, to spend with the puppies.

"I'll tell Laura about our quads, but I'll tell everyone else that you called in sick." He kissed her good-bye.

"Hey Bob," she told him, "it might be a good idea to act a little like you don't believe I'm really sick. I've been late recently, now I call in sick on a Friday. Why not let someone overhear you tell Laura that you want to see a doctor's note if I miss any more work."

"Good idea. I'll be over right after work." He leaned over the bed to give her one last delicious kiss.

She reached up, holding his face, "Stop at your house before you come over. Bring your toothbrush and enough clothes for the whole weekend and for work Monday morning. Once I have you here, you're not leaving." Her grin held pure wicked delight.

They spent the weekend together, working, making love and watching over the puppies. Bob spent a lot of time playing with Charger, who was jealous of Teddy and the litter. Once Kate overheard him talking to the male dog.

"That's what always happens with women, Buddy. They use you and then forget all about you when the babies come." He stroked Charger's sleek black head as he spoke, "Until they want more babies."

"Oh come on!" She came up behind him, sliding her arms around his waist. "That's not true!"

"Eavesdropping! Just like a woman! Here I am just having a little male bonding with the new daddy and you have to put your two cents in." He turned into her embrace. "Teddy tried to bite him."

"Well, give it a few weeks and he'll have fun playing with the puppies. He's going to love it, trust me." She laughed, "And I know men are good for more than making babies."

"Really?" he asked, innocently. "Good for what?"

"Give me time," Kate's brow furrowed as she pretended to concentrate. "I'm sure I'll think of something."

Monday, she spent the morning working at home, continuing what she had started Friday. She soon realized why they were having a hard time finding out where the shortage was coming from. There was more than one thief.

There were minor shortages from some of the cashiers at the retail outlets. It was a small amount, but the Loss Prevention team was working on the problem. Kate knew some of the cashiers were going to get a very rude awakening over the next few days. She wasn't sympathetic but she was sorry to see anyone get into so much trouble. These employees would be fired and arrested over what was really small change.

With the cashiers and their pilfering out of the way, it was easy to narrow some missing money to the girls working on cash receipts. It was a fairly steady amount, about $400.00 a month. It proved to be impossible for her to find out which of the two girls was guilty. When she got to the office that afternoon, she was still stumped.

As soon as she got to work, Bob called her into his office. "Good afternoon, my love." He kissed her gently. "How are our quads?"

"Nursing their little heads off." She smiled, "I weigh them on a food scale every day to track their growth." She began to pace around his office. "I do have something to report, just not all of it. I don't like it very much, but here goes . . ."

She went on to explain about the shortages, telling Bob that Loss Prevention was taking care of the cashiers. Then she went on to explain her evidence against one of the cash room girls and explained why she had been unable to determine which girl was behind it.

She also told him there was another one, a third thief. This was a white-collar thief, stealing through a paper trail, not cash. The third thief was the one she was brought in to catch; these others were just extras, confusing the trail.

"I feel really stupid finding out that we had several thieves on our payroll," Bob complained.

"That's not really surprising when you have eight retail outlets in this area. Every retailer knows that employee pilfering is a major loss," Kate reminded him.

"Why didn't the Loss Prevention people catch this?" Bob wondered.

"The thing is, they did catch it but the timing of their investigation and mine overlapped. I haven't met any of them, but from what I've seen, their department seems to be very well run," Kate replied. "It might be better to look at it this way, you only have a few dishonest cashiers in eight stores. That's actually a very good record, really remarkable. Loss Prevention must be responsible for that."

"Let's go through with our original plan to label you as a suspect to set up a meeting with John Wilson, the Loss Prevention department head. He'll go over your evidence and tell us what steps to take next," Bob suggested.

"Great idea, and then?" Kate was eager to get this part of it over with.

"You'll get to work at home from then on," he said gently.

"In other words, as far as everyone in the office is concerned, I'll be fired." Kate still wasn't comfortable with that part, but she grinned ruefully, "Ida will appreciate that, she's stuck puppy sitting."

"Actually, we'll just say that we sent you back to the agency. Remember, we told them you were only a temp." He noticed her silence and the look on her face, "Kate? About the cash room, whichever girl it is, you aren't responsible. Not for the trouble she'll be in. She committed the crime, not you."

"True, but I like them both. It's going to be hard to know I played a part in getting one of them arrested. Very hard." She voiced her last fear. "Another thing. What if the staff blames me? What if I lose the trust and respect of my co-workers for turning one of them in? This could turn into a real hostile working environment because they are both well liked. Who knows how much they'll like the embezzler, whoever that turns out to be."

"We'll make it clear that you were acting under orders and by solving the crimes you saved their jobs. The corporate office is getting really close to closing down this division," Bob explained.

"But not until we catch the embezzler, and that's probably going to turn out to be someone much higher up the food chain. Actually most of them are completely in the clear, unless they're accomplices. It's still hard on me." She went into his arms for a comforting hug.

"I know it is, sweetheart, it's hard on me too," Bob nodded, kissing her gently. "Now, let me call John and set up a meeting. I'll get back to you."

Kate went into her office and worked on the rather large stack of Accounts Payable paperwork that had piled up while she concentrated on investigating the shortages. To keep herself from thinking about the thefts, she really dug into the work. The best part about her using the backlog of paperwork as a distraction was that by the time she was ready to leave for the day, she was just about caught up with the payables.

Shortly before the end of the day, Bob came into her office cubicle to let her know that the meeting with John from Loss Prevention was set up for first thing in the morning.

That night, as she lay in Bob's arms, Kate finally told Bob the last part of her fears. "I've eliminated just about everyone, except for you and Laura. Either it's one of you or someone's setting you up."

"You think it's one of us?" Bob asked, as he hiked himself up on one elbow. He was clearly astonished.

"No, of course not. I trust Laura completely. There's not a dishonest bone in her body. And, I love you," she protested, sitting up and facing him.

"But I notice you left one thing out." He was hurt, and it came out sounding like an accusation. "You didn't say you trusted me."

"But trust is a part of love." She tried to still his misplaced frustration. "Of course I trust you. I just meant that the road seems to lead to one of you. I know you're both innocent but you and Laura are being set up. Someone is trying to cover his tracks by framing you. It's lucky for you that I won't fall for the frame, just because I *do* trust you."

"What if it's Laura?" he persisted. "If she's guilty, could you have her arrested?"

"It's a stupid question. It isn't her." She resisted the idea.

"All of a sudden, I think having you investigate this may not be such a good idea. You have preconceived notions." Bob got out of bed and started gathering his clothes.

"That's not true! If it is either Laura or you, when I know it, I will bring all the evidence to the right people. I'm a professional and I'm ethical. I have no respect for a thief. Bob, please permit me the basic human need to believe the best about the people I love." She loudly defended herself, "And remember there still are other suspects."

"You're right," Bob admitted.

As soon as he finished dressing, he leaned over to kiss her. "I'm sorry, I have to trust you, too. Don't I? I'm just a little stressed out right now. I hate firing people, and in the next few days we'll fire several cashiers, one of the cash room girls, and I have to pretend to fire you. What's even worse is the knowledge that the girls from the stores and the cash room will be arrested and prosecuted. I know that I have to do it, and that they deserve it but still I hate it more than you know."

"I know it's tough. I don't like it either, but they did it to themselves." She got out of bed and took him into her arms in a warm hug. "Bob, didn't you plan on staying? The kids aren't here, remember?" She punctuated these questions with a series of kisses, each a little longer and more passionate than the one before it.

"Set your alarm a little bit earlier. I forgot to bring a change of clothes so I'll have to get up early enough to go home and change." He quickly undressed again and picked her up, tossing her gently onto the bed before joining her. "I wouldn't want to be late for work."

"Don't worry about it, I washed some of the clothes you left here over the weekend. I planned on having you stay. I need you." She grinned up at him, a grin that was part minx and pure evil. "Come here, you."

Chapter Eight

Bob's smile disappeared as soon as he got to the office. The minute he stepped into the building, it hit him that soon he was going to have to fire Kate. Even though it was a charade, he realized that soon enough he would really have to fire several people. He liked and trusted everyone on his staff and it bothered him to know that in at least one person, that trust was misplaced. He began to act like a wounded grizzly bear, but was wise enough to keep away from the office staff as much as possible. He stomped into his office and slammed the door. A short time later a good-looking, tall black man came into the lobby and was directed to Bob's office. He went in and shut the door.

After a short time, Bob stuck his head out of his office and shouted, "Kate! In my office. Now!"

Kate sat still for just a moment, gathering her wits. It seemed silly to be nervous and upset about being fired when it was all a sham, but she was. She took a deep breath and stood up. It took very little acting for her face to go pale as she hurried into Bob's office. He shut the door firmly behind her.

"Kate," he said loudly, trying to be heard by anyone nosy enough to snoop around outside his door, "this is John Wilson from Loss Prevention and he wants to speak to you. Please, be seated."

Kate shook hands with John and they all sat down. She turned to John and began to tell him about the evidence she had gathered. She spoke quietly enough not to be heard outside the office.

"Actually, about the cashiers, we probably have even more

conclusive evidence on them than you realize." John continued, "As you know, we randomly videotape all the cashiers with hidden surveillance cameras. They sign a written permission to do that when they're hired. Right now, with the **Back to School** sales, and, of course," he shrugged with a cynical grin, "the back to school shoplifters, we haven't had very much time to study all the tapes. Actually a few cashiers dipping into the till for lunch change is very small potatoes compared to some we've had in the past. And, of course the cash room losses helped to cover up the cash register shortages."

"You know about the cash room losses?" Kate was surprised, she thought she was the only one to have uncovered that loss.

"Of course, we're not too stupid," John laughed. "And there is a plan, already in effect, to catch the guilty girl without letting the other girl ever know she was under suspicion. It would be much easier and faster to call them both in and question them, but it would be very painful for the innocent girl." He glanced at Bob. "I know you, Bob, and you wouldn't like it done that way."

"That's true. How are you catching the cash room thief?" Bob asked curiously.

"It's simple. We have set up a separate cash room, at security headquarters, to count the cash, and photograph all the serial numbers of any bills larger than a twenty. The people doing the extra counting are long-time employees of mine. Next, we are comparing their figures with the cash room girls' figures. The next time one of them steals anything, we'll know who she is." He paused. "Actually we already know, but we want to make sure that she's the only one involved. After all, it could turn out that they're both thieves, although I'd hate to think we missed that much when we were checking on both their references. It would sure make me review our procedure for verifying these girls' backgrounds."

"How soon will you be sure which one it is?" Kate asked,

curiously. "And that the other girl is innocent?"

"By the end of work today." He smiled. "Now I have two more questions. One, how are you doing on the paper trail?"

"I have a lead, but I have to develop it, and for that I might need your help," Kate answered, willing herself not to turn and look at Bob. "Bob and Laura have to be kept out of it."

"What?" Bob was indignant.

"Bob, I need for you to trust me this time, and let me handle this the way I feel is best," Kate told him, gently. "This doesn't mean that I suspect either of you."

"Okay, but I don't like it." He had the funniest look on his face, stubborn and a little defensive, like a little boy in trouble.

"I know you don't like it, dear. Don't pout," she grinned at him, "and don't make a face like that, you look like Sam, and he's only five." She turned back to John who was watching them with the strangest expression on his face. "What's the second question?"

"Who's that girl out in the office? Nearest the door?" he asked.

"Do you mean the receptionist?" Bob queried, "Beautiful? Young? Black? Does that describe her?"

"Yes, her," John replied. "What do you know about her?"

"Do you suspect her of something?" Bob was curious.

"Bob, don't be such an idiot," Kate added, smiling and shaking her head. "Of course he suspects her of something. He suspects her of being someone he'd like to go out with."

"Oh," Bob looked sheepish, "I get no respect, no respect at all. That's Cheryl Steedman, our receptionist. She's a very nice person, and very pretty."

"He can see that she's pretty, dummy. That's part of the reason he's asking about her." Kate added, "The important thing is that she's as pleasant as she is beautiful and she's not dating anyone right now."

"Good, she will be soon if I have anything to say about it."

John stood up, and turned to Kate. "I hate to say this, but to make this little drama look realistic, I have to go with you to your cubicle, watch as you clean out your desk and then escort you out of the building. I want them to think you're being arrested, or at least facing arrest."

"Then we'd better go." Kate looked at Bob and asked, "Will I see you later?"

"Of course, I have to bring over all the paperwork you want to study." Bob tried to seem detached and professional in front of John.

"Give it up, Bob. I'm a detective, remember? I've known Kate for about two hours and I've known you two were a couple, a couple in love, for about one hour and fifty-nine minutes." He smiled. "And she proved it when she started calling you names. You don't call someone darling and idiot in almost the same sentence if you're not in love with them."

"Unless he is a darling and an idiot." Kate winked at John, then turned to Bob. "I'll see you tonight."

"I have a better idea, you two. Let's all meet for lunch, Laura too. We could have lunch at the Plaza Hotel Grill," John suggested.

"Let's make it in about an hour. Okay, Kate?" Bob asked.

"Sure, I'm too smart to pass up a good meal." Totally ignoring John, she grabbed Bob and kissed him deeply.

John stopped her before they went out the door; he pulled something out of his pocket. It was a small plastic bottle.

"What's this?" she asked.

"Eye drops, put some in, and let it run down your cheeks, it'll make you look like you've been crying," John suggested.

She did, then she tossed back her long, red hair, took a deep breath and walked out of Bob's office. John walked alongside her, holding one of her elbows. She kept her head bowed, and her eyes lowered as she and John went into her cubicle. John stood to one side, looking stern. He watched as she grabbed the few personal items that she had on her desk, just a few pictures of her kids.

She put the items in her purse and they walked out to the car. John looked around to see if anyone was close enough to hear, then said, "I'm glad you're helping me catch the thieves, Kate, and I'm really glad to see Bob get involved with someone. You two look good together."

"Thanks. It's still kind of new, but it feels right. Heck, it feels marvelous." She got into her car. "I'll be seeing you soon."

He stood there as she drove away, and then went back to Bob's office. As expected he found the staff gathered around Bob and Laura. The women were angry and loudly demanded answers to all of their questions.

At John's suggestion, Bob made a short, simple announcement. "We didn't fire Kate; we just told the agency that we didn't need her any longer. It was because of her poor work habits, her tardiness and her high absenteeism. I liked her personally, and so did Laura. Because there have been several suspicious cash shortages, we followed the company policy, and we had John watch her clean out her desk and walk her to her car. We have no proof that she was involved in any wrongdoing, and we didn't accuse her of anything." He paused, and then added, "Yet, I know we'll need to get someone else on that desk, but for now Diana's going to handle all the payables, with Laura's help. Does anybody have any questions?"

There were several indistinct murmurs at this speech, but no outright questions. The women still seemed reluctant to get back to work so Laura suggested that they all go to lunch a little early.

"Just be back at one o'clock, ready to go back to work this afternoon, okay?" They gathered their purses and left, still muttering, leaving Bob, John and Laura behind.

Bob spoke up, "Now I know what it feels like for your employees to think you're an ogre. How about you?"

"It's part of my job," John replied. "I'm always the bad guy, somehow. It's always my fault. Thieves never will admit, even to themselves, that they caused their own problems."

"Well, it's new to me," Laura added, "and I don't like it one bit. Wait until we really have to fire someone."

"That's probably tomorrow. For now, let's go to lunch." Bob suggested, "I'm buying!"

"I guess this means I'll have to wait a while before I ask Cheryl out," John muttered, sounding disappointed.

"What's this?" Laura asked, her interest instantly aroused. "Did I miss something?"

"Not much, just that John here could use the help of a good matchmaker," Bob answered.

"Consider it done," Laura said. She turned to John with a big smile, "By the way, John are you coming to the dinner party I'm throwing Saturday night? It'll be outdoors, with a barbecue and dancing. I thought it'd be a good day for it, since we have Monday off."

"I wasn't invited, but sure, I'll come," John answered. "Will Cheryl be there?"

"Even if I have to drag her myself. By the way, no one's been invited yet. I only planned it five seconds ago, Bob?" Laura prompted.

"We'll be there," he answered.

"See? He even answers like a couple," Laura laughed. "And it's only been seventeen days since they met."

"You're counting?" Bob asked.

"Jack and I have a few bets on how things are going between you two. For example, if Kate has another baby within twelve months, I get to buy a horse." Laura laughed as she looked at him and saw the shock on his face. "You know Bob, you could really help me out here."

John took pity on Bob, who looked like he'd just had a stun gun used on him. "Back to the party. Do you mean you're throwing this party just so I can get to know Cheryl better?"

John was clearly impressed with her matchmaking efficiency.

"Count your blessings," Bob told him, recovering from his surprise at Laura's antics. "You should have seen what she did to me and Kate."

"I did not!" Laura protested. "It really was an accident, how you met her. I'm not that devious. I was going to start matchmaking when Kate started work."

"Come on, give. What happened?" John was openly curious.

"I just innocently took Kate to the beach and Bob showed up. No big deal." Laura replied guilelessly.

"Tell him which beach," Bob prompted.

"We were at the cove," she said softly.

"The nude beach?" John asked.

"That's the one," Bob smiled. "All three of us were totally naked. At first, I thought Kate was really sunburned, but she was just blushing. She was as embarrassed as the dickens. Laura was laughing her fool head off, and I didn't know what to do."

"I wasn't laughing, and you know it, you rat. But, I must admit you handled the situation very smoothly." Laura continued the story, "He invited us to his house and fixed us lunch."

"But I didn't fix enough food, apparently," he reminded her. "You and Jack had to take the kids out for ice cream after we ate. You took the kids and left me alone with Kate."

"And you and Kate got bored, left there with only each other for company, I suppose," she said archly.

"Laura, you're too ruthless. I think Cheryl's single days are numbered," John said as they walked to his car, a stunned look on his face. "And mine, too."

Bob, Laura and John met Kate for lunch at the Plaza grill, a very expensive restaurant.

"Why are we being so fancy?" Kate asked.

"Because it's way too expensive for most of the other women in the office. We don't want to be seen with you, Kate. Besides, it's on my expense account," Bob replied.

"Great. I'm a social pariah, but I get an expensive restaurant. Good enough for me," Kate laughed, feeling slightly relieved now that her public humiliation, however staged, was over. "Let's eat!"

The group ate a very good lunch. Most of them had steak, except for John who preferred Mahi Mahi. They discussed the problems at work. One tentative decision was reached. The decision over whether or not to have any of the cashiers arrested would rest with John. John was going to try to scare them into becoming honest citizens.

"We're going into the stores in two man teams, hitting all eight stores today. I'll be working with the police for the rest of the day." John relaxed a bit. "Now onto the really important stuff, who wants dessert?"

By the time Bob and Laura returned to work, they were in good spirits and ready to face the battles ahead. They had to deal with the resentful office staff, and with still being under suspicion themselves. John also had to deal with the cashiers. After that, he would finalize the investigation of the cash room girls. Kate would go home and continue following the paper trail.

John's first case was a teenager named Wendy. She was on tape taking lunch money from the till. At first, she was defiant, but it took very little for John to reduce her to tears.

He turned to her. "Here's the deal. If you sign a confession and an agreement to pay the company back in the amount of two hundred dollars, we will ask the D. A. to give you community service and probation instead of jail time. If you do not sign, we will push him to prosecute you to the fullest extent of the law. We will also sue you in civil court to collect the money, and we will try for well over four hundred dollars. We figure that you took between $5.00 and $10.00 a day for two months, and you worked an average of 20 days per month at the cash register. It's up to you which way we go."

"Why go easy on her? She's just another fatheaded thief,"

John's teammate said. "She's too stupid to deserve any mercy, and she isn't showing any remorse at all."

"I hate to admit it, but it looks like you're right," John said. "Make the call. And call her house, too. I think she still lives with her mother."

That did it, Wendy finally broke down. "No! Please don't call my mom! She'll kill me." Tears streamed down her young face.

John's teammate sat back in her chair and smiled wickedly. "Good." Her comment was quiet and chilling.

John and his partner left Wendy in the manager's office under his watchful eye.

"I think it worked." John said, "We'll know as soon as we go back in there. If she offers to pay us back out of her last paycheck, I'll believe she's really seen the light. If that happens, I will speak to the attorneys and see if she can get probation. If not, I'll recommend jail time. Either way, I call the cops, and either way, her mother gets a call." John decided, "Maybe if we do prosecute, we'll ask the D. A. to try for community service instead of jail time. I do think she's, uh, worth salvaging. What do you think?"

"Let's get back to it," his partner said.

When they got back to the manager's office, Wendy did what John had hoped. She offered to pay back the money that she had stolen from her final paycheck. The store manager cashed it, and brought her the change. Since she was under eighteen, John called Wendy's mother and told her about the thefts, and why Wendy was fired. He also told her how Wendy had repaid the money from her final check. She promised to have a long talk with Wendy when the girl got home. A noticeably changed girl stopped and looked back at them as she walked out the door.

"I know you don't believe this, but I'm sorry," Wendy sniffed.

"Sure, you're sorry because you got caught," John said. "But why weren't you sorry before you got caught and fired? Why did you do it in the first place? And most important of all, did you learn something or will you do this again?"

"I won't do this again, you'll see," the girl promised as she left.

"I give it a fifty-fifty chance. But I think sending her to jail wouldn't help the odds either way. She hasn't heard the last of this. The way her mother sounded on the phone, she's going to be sorrier still." John said tightly, "I'm not a psychic but eighteen or not, I see a bright red bottom in that girl's future."

"Good," his partner said.

When he got outside his cell phone rang. It was Kate.

"John? How will I be able to go to Laura's party Saturday? Won't Cheryl think it's strange if I'm there after supposedly being sent away from the office in complete disgrace?" she asked.

"We'll have to solve everything by then, or ask Bob if he feels that he can take Cheryl into his confidence." John smiled, "This is Tuesday, I hope by Friday you'll know who the thief is. And remember, I'm taking care of the cash room losses."

"I still need to meet with you, away from the office, and without Bob," she said firmly.

"You don't suspect him?" John asked with a hint of shock.

"Of course not, or Laura either. I do, however, feel that the person I do suspect is trying to point the blame on one of them and away from himself." Kate smiled, "And while I have the experience to follow the paper trail, I don't know how to gather hard evidence. That's where you come in."

"Okay, I'll come over to your house first thing in the morning." John wrote down her address and they set a time.

"John, you used to be a cop, didn't you?" Kate had mischief in her voice.

"Yes."

"Good, then you bring the donuts," she laughed openly as she disconnected the call.

As soon as Kate got home she went in to look at the puppies.

Ida sat beside her on the floor. They talked to Teddy and gently stroked the little puppies. They were almost a week old and already too cute for words. Ida asked her several gentle but probing questions about Bob and her new job before she left to get ready for her date that night with George.

When she could finally tear herself away from the litter Kate visited with Charger, giving him some extra love and attention before she settled down to work.

It was ludicrous, she thought to herself, she sometimes felt guilty about going to work late so many times and her poor attendance record. Most of the staff would probably agree. The truth, she had to keep reminding herself, was completely different. The truth was that if she added up all the work she had done from her home, the company would owe her a lot of overtime pay. She wouldn't get it until everything was solved but she had already planned to put a down payment on a newer van. With air conditioning that worked, and a good stereo, and . . .

She pulled her attention back to the reports in front of her. She went over her figures from the day before and came to the same conclusion. She hoped she was right. More than that, she knew she was right. She had to be.

The alternative was unthinkable.

Chapter Nine

The next morning John arrived on her doorstep with a dozen donuts. Kate made coffee and they sat at the kitchen table. After the dogs greeted John and managed to weasel several bites of donut from both of them, they were banished to the backyard. However when they scratched at the door to get back in, Kate shut Teddy in the den with her litter and left Charger outside.

Kate spread out her paperwork on the table. She asked John if he would fill her in on the problems in the cash room.

"We traced the money and we're satisfied that there is only one culprit. The other woman is completely innocent." John sipped his coffee. "And this time the guilty one will go to jail. This is no stupid, rebellious teenager; this is a woman who has betrayed a position of trust."

"Which one was it?" She thought about both of the women. She hadn't spent as much time with them as she had with the other office girls, but she liked them.

Sherry was tall and slender, Hispanic with long, chocolate hair. She was always smiling and full of energy. She was single and liked to talk about her boyfriend. Tonya was more quiet, a short curvy brunette, who seemed to care only about her two kids.

"Tonya. When her husband left her she got desperate and stupid. Instead of trying to get child support from him, she began to steal from us. One of our problems was that we couldn't see anything she was spending money on. There was no extravagant shopping or drugs. No wild lifestyle. She was using what she stole to pay her rent and feed her kids," John said. "But I don't feel sorry for her. If she had come to us, any one of several things could have been done to help. The company would have offered her low-cost legal services, credit counseling, even help in finding a nice apartment with lower rent. Hell, she was even due for a raise and a promotion in two months. You know Bob, if she had gone to him, he would have helped her."

"Of course he would have." Kate was still saddened at the thought of what this would do to Tonya and her kids. "But what will happen to her family now that she'll be fired? And arrested."

"Those kids are her only hope for any mercy at all. Bob and the regional manager have been worried about the kids." John grabbed a second donut. "But we have to prosecute. We have no choice."

Just then the doorbell rang. It was Shelly, the girl she had been working with over the phone.

"Hi! I'm Kate, it's nice to finally meet you," she greeted the very pregnant girl. "Come on in. Do you know John?"

"I've heard of him but we've never met." Shelly followed Kate and they made their way into the kitchen. She looked at John and greeted him. "Hi."

"Hi, you must be Shelly, it's nice to meet you. Sit down and have a donut." John looked her over.

Shelly was pale with long blond hair and big blue eyes. She looked about eighteen but John knew she was twenty-five. She was also very near the end of her pregnancy, and huge. She was in a loose flowing dress.

"Would you like some milk?" Kate asked her. "Or anything else?"

"I think I'll skip eating, I've been feeling a little weird all day," Shelly replied.

"There's a word that sometimes applies to feeling weird at this time in your pregnancy, it's called labor," Kate told her, smiling. "Are you sure you want to work on this today?"

"If I don't do it now, you're gonna have to wait a few weeks," Shelly smiled. "But I'm sure I'm not in labor, it's just wishful thinking. In fact, I'm positive I'm going to be pregnant forever."

"Believe me, I know the feeling," Kate grinned. "Nine months doesn't sound very long but believe me, it's an eternity. But it's worth it."

"Oh, yeah." Shelly gently ran her hand over the swell of her belly. "Well worth it."

The trio got to work. Kate showed them both where and how she thought the money was being embezzled. Shelly helped her arrange the reports and papers she was showing to John. Then John took over and explained what steps he would use to gather evidence to convict the thief. Because of the way the thief had covered his tracks, it was still impossible to prove which of three people was really guilty. Two of those three people were Bob and Laura, the third possibility was the purchasing manager, Jerry Weisner.

It was almost noon when John gathered up the papers he needed and got ready to leave. He seemed reluctant to go to the office.

"I have to go in this afternoon and deal with the cash room problem," he said heavily. "It's the part of this job I really hate."

Shelly was also ready to leave. She was almost to the door when she stopped and turned to Kate, "Remember when I said it wasn't labor? I may have miscalculated slightly. I hope." Her eyes were wide with anticipation.

"It never fails, whenever I get close to solving this, I wind up going to the hospital." Kate was amused. "First, Teddy and now you."

"Who's Teddy? And why did he have to go to the hospital?" Shelly asked curiously.

"Teddy's a she, and John already met her this morning. Come on, I'll show you." She led the two into the den where Teddy was resting quietly with her puppies. "There's why she went to the hospital." She gestured to the four puppies sleeping next to Teddy. "She couldn't be a normal dog, she had to have a c-section."

"Oh! They're adorable. How old are they?" Shelly asked.

"Six days." Kate smiled as she always did when she looked at the puppies.

"Are you going to sell them?" John knelt down and stretched out his hand, letting Teddy smell him. "Is it all right to pick one up?"

"Sure. They'll bring about $800.00 each. I have to sell three. I can only keep one puppy." She picked up the little female who had already become her favorite. "This one."

John cuddled one and handed it to Shelly. He looked until he found the little male. "I want this little guy. Is he spoken for yet?"

"He is now," she told him. "He'll be a lucky dog. But you can't have him for about seven more weeks."

Shelly stroked the little female John had handed her. "Let me speak to my husband before you promise this little dear to anyone else. Oh!" Her eyes got big. "I definitely miscalculated. This is labor." She checked her watch. "Five minutes."

"This meeting is now officially declared over, I'll drive you to the hospital and call your husband from there. John, you go on to the office, we'll call you later." Kate took charge.

John gave her a jaunty salute, "Oui, Mon Capitan."

He helped her get Shelly safely into the car just before he left to go to the office and deal with Tonya. He leaned in Kate's car window and winked at Shelly, "Want to trade places?"

Just then another labor pain hit her and she smiled weakly, "I'm willing if you are." .

Kate turned to Shelly, "What hospital?"

"Valley General." Shelly was relaxing now, the pain had passed.

Kate drove Shelly to the hospital and waited until her husband came rushing in. She introduced herself to him.

"Don't worry so much," she told him. "This is going to be

the best day of your life. Believe me, I know. The only problem you might have is the one I'll give you if you don't remember to call me and let me know if it's a boy or a girl. Here's my number, now go hug your wife."

She handed him the slip of paper with her phone number on it and then left, repeating her instructions for him to call her as soon as anything happened.

Kate knew the day was going to be hard on Bob. He was a caring and considerate man who didn't like to fire any of his people. Having Tonya arrested was going to be doubly hard on him. She decided to spend the evening cheering him up. After thinking up a plan, she called Bob at the office.

"Hey, lover. What's up?" she asked, sounding cheerful.

"So far today, nothing. I miss having you here, and I hate the idea of firing Tonya. I'm sitting here with her final check in front of me, and John has already called the police." He was down. "We're trying to arrest her quietly without upsetting the whole office. John asked for plain-clothes officers to come and take her downtown for booking."

"What about her kids?" Kate asked sadly.

"I don't know yet," Bob told her. "I know she did this to herself but it's sad. Her future is ruined and she'll do time."

"You want to cheer up? Shelly is in labor," Kate informed him. "I just talked to her husband and they told him it would be any time now. Also, I've had two puppies spoken for."

"Let me guess, Shelly and John? I should have warned Shelly that going to your house causes the onset of labor."

Kate laughed. "We'd better hope not, remember?"

"True." Bob sounded rueful. "What else is up?"

"Well, I had an idea. I thought I could go to your house and relax by the pool. Is that okay?" she asked.

"Sure, no problem." He thought of something. "But you don't have a key."

"Funny, that's why I called." She smiled as she thought of

her plan. "Do you have one hidden around the house or with a neighbor?"

"Yeah, the woman in the green house next door has my spare key. I'll call her and tell her to let you in," he told her.

"Can Charger come?" she asked.

"Sure. I just wish I as going to be there," he sounded resigned, "instead of stuck here."

"Well, maybe I'll stay until you get home," Kate hinted. "Maybe I'll have some wine on ice and something ready to throw on the barbecue."

"Maybe I'll be home as soon as I can. Wear a sexy swimsuit for me." He hung up and got back to work.

Bob held a short meeting with Laura, giving her instructions for handling the office for the rest of the day. Then he called in John and they discussed their meeting with Tonya, going over the way they wanted to handle things. Finally Bob called Tonya into his office.

Tonya entered the office looking tired and apprehensive. Bob introduced her to John and told her that John was the head of Loss Prevention. As soon as he finished introducing John, Tonya began to cry.

"I knew it! You know, don't you? About the money I've been taking," Tonya sobbed. "I had to! I had to take the money. My husband walked out and didn't leave me a dime. He hasn't even sent any child support. What was I supposed to do?"

"Why didn't you just come to me and let me try to help you?" Bob asked her. "I can understand how you might be desperate, but you didn't even give me a chance. It hurts that you didn't come to me. Is it easier to steal than to ask for help?"

"I was afraid to ask, afraid that if you turned me down I'd have to take the money anyway. Once you knew how desperate I was, I'd be the first person you'd suspect." Tonya had stopped sobbing quite as much, but she was still sniffling. John silently handed her a box of tissues.

"Didn't you realize that you'd be putting Sherry under suspicion? Was that fair to her?" Bob asked.

"No, it wasn't fair to her," Tonya admitted, then raised her voice, "but who ever said life was fair? Was it fair for my husband to walk out and leave me with two kids? With no child support? To run up the charge cards and clean out the bank account?"

The intercom buzzed. "Yes Cheryl?" He hated the interruption and his voice was curt.

"There are two men here from the police to see you." Her voice was full of suppressed curiosity.

"Send them in." His voice was curt as Bob met Tonya's eyes squarely with his own. "The police are here. They're here to arrest you for the thefts. Is there anyone who can take care of your kids until you make bail?"

"My mother can watch them. She has them now." Tonya sobbed, "Bob, I know I don't deserve it but can you help me? Please? Is there any way I can make restitution and avoid being arrested?"

"No, corporate insisted on your arrest. If you agree to make full restitution I can ask the D. A. to plead the case out and seek a sentence of probation and community service. That's the best I could do. However, I want you to be sure of one thing: I'm doing this for your kids. Otherwise I would push for as long a sentence as I could get."

Tonya sagged in her chair and renewed her weeping. John came over to her and gently but firmly told her that if she cooperated, she wouldn't have to face the public humiliation of being handcuffed and led out of Bob's office. He told her he was going along to press formal charges against her and to give the police the evidence that they had against her. He wanted to know if she had a lawyer she could call. Tonya just shook her head weakly and walked out with the police and John.

The women in the office were buzzing. To them this was the

second person fired that week. They were angry and worried. Although he would have preferred to keep quiet on the subject, Bob made an announcement.

"I'm sure you noticed Tonya leaving with John from Loss Prevention." Bob paused. "I don't want to comment on this, but I feel you have the right to know what's happening. Please remember that nothing has been proven in court. There were irregularities in the cash room reports that we traced to Tonya. We are completely satisfied no one else was involved. We turned all of our evidence over to the police. The amounts and frequencies of the company losses were such that the police will investigate and follow up." He drew a deep breath, and for a brief moment his expression was unguarded so that the staff could see the stress and strain written on his face.

He continued, "No one regrets this more than I do, but there was no other way to handle it. I know that coming so soon after letting Kate go you are upset and angry with me, and probably wondering who's next. All I can say is that I had no choice in either case. Now, I'm going home early. Laura's in charge for the rest of the day. Listen, I know you're all upset. So am I. If anyone has any questions or problems to discuss with me, we'll talk them out tomorrow." Bob went back into his office before leaving for home.

Kate made herself busy at Bob's place. She put some chicken breasts in a marinade, getting them ready to barbecue, and then she made a salad and refrigerated the wine, a crisp Chablis. Besides the chicken and salad, she had fresh French rolls and corn on the cob.

She made sure the largest raft Bob owned was fully inflated and in the pool. The raft was a large mattress the size of a double bed. She set the picnic table with a red and white checkered tablecloth, Bob's best china and flatware, and crystal wine goblets. Then she made herself a large pitcher of ice water, and put it on the deck of the pool next to a paperback romance she was reading. She took a long look around the large yard, noticing the high fence. She made her decision. She undressed and gingerly got onto the raft.

The raft drifted away from the side of the pool as she got onto it. Using one hand, she idly paddled over to the edge to grab her book and get a sip of cold water. When she reached for the book, Charger came over and licked her right on the end of her nose.

Laughing, she pushed off and just let the raft drift. If she got close enough to touch a side of the pool, she pushed off gently and kept drifting. Charger ran around the edge trying to figure out where she was going to land next. That was how Bob found her when he got home.

He stopped and gazed at her with amusement. "Ahem! I see you're wearing my favorite bathing suit again."

She looked at her naked body, smiling impishly, "This old thing? I've had it since the day I was born."

"I think it's changed a bit." Bob took off his clothes and jumped in swimming a few laps. He swam over to where she was holding the raft next to the edge. "Will this thing hold both of us?"

"I don't know, but if you start to drown I'll rescue you," she wiggled her eyebrows, "mouth to mouth."

Slowly and carefully, he got onto the large raft. He lay beside her and took her into his arms. She threw the book over onto the deck where Charger picked it up. He ran around the pool for a while with the book in his mouth.

"I didn't know Charger was a romance reader," Bob joked.

"Nora Roberts gets 'em every time." Kate lowered her mouth to his.

They cuddled for a long time, talking quietly and kissing softly until she felt the tension from his day leaving him.

Kate nibbled his neck, then gradually turned her attention to his chest. Moving slowly and carefully on the precarious raft, she used her hands and mouth to explore his nipples. One hand moved down his abdomen. Bob carefully began his own exploration, first with his hands on her breasts, then he slid his hands lower still. He pulled her back up to his mouth and he kissed her, a kiss full of passion that just about made the pool turn to steam.

Trying not to sink the raft, moving slowly, he maneuvered himself over her body. She spread her legs and he entered her. He began to move within her slowly and ever so carefully. As their passion increased, they picked up the pace. Suddenly they realized that their luck had run out, there was a hole in the raft and they were sinking.

Luckily, the raft was in the shallow end. Bob touched bottom and walked over to the side of the pool, his hands under Kate's bottom, holding her up. She had her arms wrapped around his neck, her legs around his waist. Without his mouth ever leaving hers, without his manhood ever leaving her femininity, he let go of her behind and grabbed the side of the pool, one hand on either side of her head. They both ignored Charger who came over to lick Bob's hands and the back of Kate's head before going back to lie down in the last little spot of sun. At the side of the pool they slowed the pace of their lovemaking. They were still standing in the shallow end, with Bob still bracing himself at the side of the pool. They made love slowly then built up once again, this time coming to a climax that left them both gasping.

"I guess we know now, it is possible to make love on the raft." Kate sighed. "At least until we get carried away by passion."

"Is there any other way for us to make love? I wonder if the inflatable dolphin would work even better," Bob speculated.

"Or maybe that extra large inner tube?" she suggested. "It's getting cool, let's experiment another day. Why don't you start the barbecue and while the coals are getting just right, we can take a nice warm shower?"

"A pleasurable, very long, warm shower?" He kissed her.

"Goes without saying. Anything worth doing is worth doing right." She broke away from his kiss. "As long as we're warm."

She went into the house, heading for the master bath off Bob's bedroom. It was the first time she had been in Bob's bedroom; she noted the off-white walls and a massive oak bed with a royal blue comforter.

Bob lit the charcoal and followed her inside. He found her adjusting the temperature of the shower. They took a long shower, gently soaping, teasing and exploring each other's bodies. Barely stopping to dry off, they moved to the bed, stripped off the blue velour comforter and made love again. The lovemaking this time was more tender than it had been in the pool, but just as passionate. Afterwards, they lay there for a short time, letting their heart rates slow down and getting their breathing under control.

Finally, with a kiss and a hug, Kate prodded him out of bed. "Go out there and cook the chicken, I'll get the rest of dinner."

"Do we have to?" Bob resisted getting out of bed and began to kiss her neck.

"Yes, we have to," she told him firmly, "but we can come back here for dessert."

Bob got out of bed and pulled on some shorts and a T-shirt. Kate pulled on a skirt and a silky shell blouse. They went into the kitchen. She got the chicken out of the refrigerator and gave it to him to cook on the grill. Then she got the salad ready and found the salad dressing, wrapped the corn in foil for the grill, put butter on the table, and warmed up a few rolls in the microwave. Finally, she opened the chilled wine.

While they waited for the chicken to cook, they ate their salads and some of the rolls. Before they got the chicken off the grill, she tied Charger up to Bob's fence. The little dog laid down and whined softly, looking punished.

"Do you have to?" Bob asked.

"Yes I have to. He begs," Kate told him, "but there should be plenty of chicken for him to have later. That is if you want to feed it to him. Deal?"

"Deal." He smiled.

They ate in a companionable silence, enjoying the late summer evening and the food. By the time they gave Charger his paper plate loaded with chicken they were both relaxed and content.

"Well, boss, I hope I raised your spirits," Kate quipped.

"You know exactly what you raised, and how. I noticed one thing tonight, you didn't blush," he pointed out.

"Why should I blush? It was only you." Kate grinned at him. "Let's get these dishes into the dishwasher."

Working together they cleaned up the kitchen. Then they went into the den and watched a movie Kate had rented. It was a popular, romantic comedy and it was good, but by the end they had turned their attention to each other. The phone rang and Bob answered it. When he hung up he turned to Kate, a large smile on his face.

"Shelly had a girl, 7 pounds 1 ounce, they don't have the name picked out yet," he told her.

"That's great!" Kate kissed him. "Let's go see her tomorrow."

"I'd love to. Let's celebrate." He kissed her. "I want some ice cream."

"I could force myself to eat a bowl," she admitted.

They went into the kitchen and made huge ice cream sundaes for themselves. They both preferred vanilla ice cream, but Kate wanted hot fudge while Bob went for chocolate syrup. They used a mountain of whipped cream. Kate grabbed the Oreos, crumbling a few on top of both sundaes over the whipped cream.

Some of the ice cream and syrup accidentally spilled onto the floor. Bob looked up, a guilty but phony grin on his face.

"You remind me of Sam," Kate said. "And chocolate's not

good for dogs, but I guess that little bit can't hurt." She opened the door and called Charger, then with an impish grin she squirted a small amount of whipped cream onto the floor with the ice cream.

"So I'm a pushover, too. Let's be sinfully decadent and eat these in bed," she suggested, picking up her bowl.

"Sounds wicked to me." Bob grabbed his bowl.

He didn't notice that she smuggled the rest of the whipped cream upstairs with her. What followed was the total ruination of two pillowcases and a bottom sheet. It was glorious. Ice cream wound up on Bob's chest, so Kate cleaned it off with her tongue. Whipped cream wound up on Kate's breasts, stomach, and even lower. It took Bob a long time to get it all off Kate since he was very thorough. By the time he was finished Kate was limp.

Some of the ice cream was even consumed out of the bowls. Still it continued, chocolate and warm fudge sauce, blended with cool ice cream that was just beginning to melt, on various parts of their two bodies. Tongues were busy trying to keep it from being wasted and from spreading to the sheets. Finally, replete, they managed to get out of bed, change the sheets, and then drag themselves to the shower.

"Bob, are we getting old?" Kate teased him, "We used to have so much fun in the shower. Now all I want to do is get clean."

"I guess we've gone from swingers to old fuddy-duddies in the last few hours then. I never thought old age would hit me so fast," Bob mused. "It only took a half-gallon of ice cream and several gallons of chocolate syrup."

"And whipped cream," Kate added.

"And great sex." He kissed her.

"Especially great sex," she murmured.

They got out of the shower and dried off. Finally they were ready for bed.

Once in it, Bob kissed Kate on the shoulder and said, "Kate?

Who's watching the puppies?"

"Ida volunteered to stay over with them," she replied. "They're almost big enough to leave overnight, but I'm a worrywart."

"So Ida knows you're staying here?" Bob was surprised and more than a little uncomfortable with the idea.

"She suggested it. I was only coming over for dinner," Kate snuggled closer to him, "and to cheer you up."

"Remind me to send her roses." Bob gave Kate a plaintive look, "Kate, can I?"

"You're such a softy, that may be why I love you." She kissed him. "Go on."

She sat up and watched him get out of bed, enjoying the sight with frank admiration. He left the room and returned a few minutes later with Charger. With the little male dog curled up at the foot of the bed, finally they drifted off to sleep.

Chapter Ten

When the alarm rang the next morning, they were still cuddled in each other's arms. Bob kissed her gently on the lips, and then as she opened her mouth to his, the kiss flared until the lovers were swept away by passion. She slid her hand under the covers and reached for him.

"How soon do you have to be at work?" she asked breathlessly, her mouth warm against his.

"Too soon," Bob sighed, his voice gritty with regret, "and it's going to be a rough day. Have I said thank you?"

"What for?" Kate's mouth moved down to nibble on his neck.

"For all the things you did last night, making dinner for me, listening to me, giving me emotional support, raising my spirits, reminding me that life is fun, and . . ." He paused, eyes glinting.

Each of the items on his list had been punctuated with a kiss, one on her nose, one on her brow, one on her chin, one on her neck, and the last on her breast.

"And. . ." she prompted.

"And the ice cream." He lowered his mouth to hers, taking her lower lip with his teeth and gently sucking on it. Finally he raised his mouth just a bit, "But especially, thank you for the great sex, although it was more than sex, it was making love."

"I suspect it was good old-fashioned sex in the pool, and pure wicked decadence with the ice cream. But it was definitely lovemaking in the bed." Kate pulled him back to her mouth, "And isn't it lucky we're still in bed? Can't you be a little late? Remember, you're the boss."

With his mouth against hers, he muttered, "I guess I could at that. But I've been late a lot lately."

"So change the office hours," she quipped. "But seriously, when were you late?"

He thought about it. "Actually, *you're* the one who was late so often. I've only been late once lately. Last Thursday, the morning after you dragged me up the stairs and ravaged me."

"As I recall, it wasn't that hard to accomplish." She smiled at the memory.

And those were the last coherent words either of them spoke for a very long time. They were cuddling for a few last precious seconds when the bedside phone rang. Bob picked it up.

After listening to it for a few minutes, he said, "Yes, Ma'am, I'm very honored." He handed the phone to Kate, looking slightly dazed.

"Kate dear, it's Ida. I just thought I'd call to let you know your friend Laura is trying to get in touch with you. I didn't tell her where you were," Ida said with a touch of pride. "And sake's alive, that girl is persistent."

"Thanks, Ida. She'll probably guess where I am anyway, the brat," Kate said. "By the way, thanks for staying with the puppies. If Teddy's been fed, you can leave them alone. I'll be home soon." She waited, listening, "Thanks again, I'll see you soon."

Kate looked at Bob, "Does it bother you that Ida knows about us?"

"I was a little afraid that might resent a new man in your life but she seems to have accepted me." He gazed at Kate. "She said that for as long as you and I were together, I was an honorary member of her family."

"Even now that she has George, she's still lonesome. Remember, she lost her son and her husband within three months of each other," Kate sighed.

"That must have been rough," he said with compassion, planting a gentle kiss on her forehead. "On both of you."

"Yeah, Greg, my father-in-law, was a great guy." Kate sighed, "I really loved him."

Kate dialed the phone, calling Laura. "Hi brat. I heard you were trying to find me."

"And I heard you weren't home at seven in the morning? Where have you been?" Laura questioned.

"I was out, uh, busy, um, tied up, well, I'm here now. What doing?" she asked, using one of their old phrases.

"I'd like to know what *you're* doing. Anyway, I've got to go to the doctor's this morning, so I thought we could meet for lunch afterwards," she invited.

"Sounds like a plan." Kate asked, "Is everything all right with the baby?"

"Well, remember the news I gave you about two weeks ago? That was from a home test kit. Now, I want to go get the word straight from the doctor's mouth. It makes it more official," Laura told her. "I have to go now, I'd better call Bob and tell him I'm going to be leaving for a long lunch around ten."

"Hold on, don't freak out, okay? Here," Kate handed the phone to Bob, "she wants to talk to you."

"Hi Laura," he said, then he held the phone away from his ear for several seconds. "She freaked out," he laughed.

Both Bob and Kate could hear strange sounds coming from the phone.

Finally Bob brought the mouthpiece close enough to his mouth to say, "What's up?" He listened for a while, "Sure, no problem. I might be a little late today. I should be there before you have to leave. Yeah, thanks. Here she is."

Kate listened for a while. "No, what makes you say that? No. Remember, I already told you, I was tied up. All night." She hung up laughing.

"What was that?" Bob asked.

"Laura wanted to know all about our love life, you know, the juicy details. I told her I didn't know what she meant. We weren't doing anything sexy. I said you just kept me tied up all night." Kate laughed again. "I don't think she believed me."

"I should hope not." Bob started to get ready for work, then leaned over to give her a quick kiss. "I would never tie you up. A playful spanking maybe, but never tie you up. I like what you do when your hands are free too much for that."

"Like this?" Kate got out of bed and walked over to him.

She put her arms around his neck, pulling him to her for a longer kiss. Her lips parted as they met his. Her hands slid off his neck and trailed down his chest, raking his nipples lightly with her manicured nails.

"That works for me." Bob broke off the kiss. "Too well, I'm already going to be late for work, so help me out here, please?"

Bob walked into his bathroom and turned on the shower. Kate, feeling slightly rejected even though she knew it was illogical, pulled on her skirt and blouse, and went downstairs to make breakfast. She made toast, coffee, orange juice and bacon. Then she went up to Bob's bathroom and stuck her head into his shower.

"How do you want your eggs, handsome?" she asked.

"Later." He pulled her, clothes and all into the shower and kissed her. Their tongues met in a gentle loving duel. He peeled her wet shorts down her legs, but before he peeled her blouse off he got distracted by her hard nipples clearly visible through the wet material. He played a teasing game, nibbling, suckling and even nipping them.

"You rat!" She pretended to be angry, an act that was ruined by her breathless gasps. "Now what am I going to wear home?"

"A big smile." His mouth met hers again, and his hands went to the buttons of her blouse, finally stripping it off. "A very big smile."

"That ought to make the traffic cops happy." She locked her arms around the back of his neck, but she pretended to pout. "I thought you wanted to get to work. I thought I was making you too late."

"I'm a fool," Bob admitted.

She looked up into his eyes with a tender smile on her face, "Yes. I thought that, too."

She never did get around to making eggs. She got out of the shower, put on a robe and put her clothes in Bob's dryer. They sat at the table and ate cold toast and bacon for breakfast. When he couldn't put it off, Bob left for work. Incredibly he was only slightly over an hour late.

Kate retrieved her clothes from the dryer and went home. She turned Charger loose and went in to greet Teddy and the four puppies. The puppies' little eyes were just starting to open, and they seemed so big and fat she could swear they had gained weight overnight. Then she put on a bright green dress and got ready to meet Laura for lunch.

Laura's doctor appointment was for 10:30, so Kate figured she'd probably really see the doctor around noon, with luck. She thought she'd meet Laura at the restaurant about 12:30. She was surprised when Laura called her at 11:30 and said she had already seen the doctor and was leaving for the restaurant.

"I don't believe your doctor was actually sticking to her schedule. I always wind up waiting well over an hour," Kate told Laura, hugging her when they met at the restaurant. "You look great! Is that a new dress?"

Laura had on a red dress with a full flowing skirt. It looked fresh and would never be out of style.

"Yes. Do you like it? It's probably going to be my last non-maternity dress for a while. Well, my doctor surprised me, too. She said it was the first morning in two months without any emergencies, babies to deliver, or last minute patients. In fact, she had time to really talk with me." Laura smiled. "I think she was almost as happy about that as I was. She warned me not to get spoiled however; it's usually a madhouse in her office."

"So? Did she confirm your pregnancy?" Kate asked, "Is it

really official?"

"Yes." Laura's face lit up with excitement. "She said I'm about nine weeks along."

Kate hugged her friend, "In that case, lunch is on me. And I might even answer some of the questions I know you're going to ask."

"Who me?" Laura asked innocently before launching into an interrogation that would have made J. Edgar Hoover proud.

Kate ate her lunch and good-naturedly fielded her friend's questions. By the time Laura had finished lunch and started heading back to the office, she had a fairly good idea of how Kate and Bob's relationship was going. In fact, she was taking full credit as the matchmaker, and had volunteered to be the maid of honor.

"It's a little early to start planning the wedding, dear. I just met the man." Kate paid for lunch and walked with her out to her car.

"It's never too early to hope, is it?" Laura asked her with a saucy grin.

"I guess not. Laura, how were the women in the office acting this morning? I mean, were they still resentful of Bob because of Tonya?" Kate was concerned.

"They would have taken it much better if you hadn't been ushered out in apparent disgrace just two days earlier. Now, they seem to think this is going to be a regular occurrence. Heads will roll! Unexplained disappearances! Wholesale slaughter! Film at eleven!" Laura intoned dramatically then she sighed, "They act like we've been replaced by pods. Remember that old movie *Invasion of the Body Snatchers*? You think they'd realize that we must have had a good reason for our actions. We've always been more than fair with them. I'm starting to get mad right back at them because we deserve a little of their faith."

"They'll come around. This is just a knee-jerk reaction." Kate reassured her, "I know they all like and respect both of you.

So get back to work, boss. I hope to be back soon. And Shelly's coming back in three months, at least part-time." She laughed, "Tell Bob I miss him, its been almost three hours. And tell him I'll be at my house."

Bob came over right after work. He seemed tense and distracted as he kissed Kate at the door. He went in to see the puppies. Kate got an old blanket out and spread it on the living room rug. Then she got two cold beers and opened them. She told Bob to bring the puppies into the living room. Bob put the puppies on the blanket, then they both sat on the floor and drank their beer. Somehow watching them, their innocent clumsiness and play, made all the tensions of the day fade away.

The puppies were still small and awkward, with their little eyes just starting to open. They were barely beginning to move around, but in spite of that they were starting to play. They had little mock fights and crawled all over each other. Teddy ignored her litter and went outside for a while. Charger sat by Kate and watched them curiously; this was the closest he'd ever been to the puppies. Occasionally he put his short pug nose down and smelled, licked or even pushed one of them. Teddy came back in and immediately all the little guys started to nurse.

"Tell me about your day," Kate prompted. "Did the peasants revolt or did you manage to reassure them?"

"I had private meetings with each and every one of them. I think I've smoothed any ruffled feathers, except Rita. She's still talking about staging a revolution." Bob was worried, "I don't know if I can ever make peace with her. And Cheryl is acting even stranger, she's almost too calm and accepting. It's weird."

"When this is over, maybe I can help," Kate offered. "Will this change the plans for the party?"

"No, that's still on. Don't argue," he put a finger over her lips, just as she parted them to speak, "you're coming, even if it means we let people in on our secret before we originally planned too."

"What if Cheryl doesn't show up? If she's upset with you and Laura, she might not come." Kate worried.

"In our private meeting today I made her promise to come. I even hinted that I had a surprise for her." Bob grinned, "Her feminine curiosity will get her there."

Kate slugged his arm playfully, "Chauvinist! Isn't she suspicious that she's the only one from the office invited?"

"Originally that was my plan," Bob admitted. "To make her curious."

"You, my love, are a devious devil." She kissed him, "But you said it was part of your original plan, what's changed?"

"I've talked with John and Laura, we may be able to have the whole staff at her party, and still have you there." He drained his beer. "It's kind of a good news, bad news situation."

"What's the good news?" she asked hopefully.

"It looks like Laura and I are going to be in the clear," he said, kissing her.

"That's fantastic. What's the bad news?" She nibbled on his neck.

"We've got a major hang-up. The police and our own investigators are having trouble gathering the necessary evidence. My name is on a lot of suspicious documents, but the handwriting, like my signature, doesn't seem to be a match. They think I'm in the clear, but they're not sure. The same with Laura, except that she's more in the clear than I am because her name is on less of the dubious documents, and the signatures don't match her writing at all." Bob drew a deep breath, "On top of all that, Jerry Weisner is missing."

"Doesn't that incriminate him?" She pulled back to look at him.

"Not if he was made to disappear." Bob sighed deeply, "So his disappearance can go either way, for me or against me."

"It's ridiculous! What do they think you did? Murder Jerry to cover up embezzling money?" Bob shrugged, his face carefully blank.

Kate continued, "That's not only ridiculous, it's completely ludicrous. Why would you do something so stupid? There wasn't enough money involved to make it worth murder. I mean, if you were the kind who could murder someone anyway, which you're not."

"There's well over a hundred thousand dollars involved, plus the threat of prison and public disgrace," Bob reminded her. "People have killed for less. Much less."

"Nonsense, Jerry knows he's about to be arrested and he's bolted." Kate said sternly, "They'll catch him."

"Some of the questions brought out by Jerry's disappearance involve just that point. How does he know he's about to be arrested? What has he got to hide? There's even a possibility he might know about you. The police think that if he does know you were the inside investigator, you could be in danger." Bob was serious. "So be careful."

"Danger? From Jerry Weisner? He was always so polite and, um, jovial. That sounds too strange to be real. They'll catch him soon and solve this case." She kissed him, pushing him down to the carpet.

"But not soon enough for me." He met her passion with his own, then began to laugh as he felt several little feet trying to climb on him. "I'm being invaded!"

"Maybe it's time to put these little guys back in their box. Then," she added firmly, "we'll find something to eat. That way, after dinner we can concentrate on pleasing each other for the rest of the night."

"Sounds like a plan to me," he agreed.

"Then grab a puppy or two and follow me," she instructed.

Soon the puppies were safely ensconced back in their box, with Teddy in attendance. They each settled down for a long puppy nap. Kate and Bob made their way into the kitchen and began to dig into the refrigerator.

"I have two steaks," Kate told him, "and some brown rice. Or I can make hamburgers with fries and milkshakes. What do you think?"

"Steak. I'm not letting you near ice cream again until I recover from last night. And what you do with whipped cream is..."

"Sinful?" she suggested.

"Wonderful." Bob kissed her deeply. "And sinful."

"But you need to recover?" She teased him, "I have proof now, you're getting old. Okay, I'll fix the steaks and rice, but you're in charge of salads and rolls."

"Wait until after dinner, you'll pay for those remarks. Old!" He walked by her pausing only to give her a smart slap on her round derriere.

"Chauvinist pig!" she squealed. "Why do I put up with you?"

"Because you love me?" Bob nibbled on the back of her neck.

"It only goes to prove it; there's no accounting for taste." She leaned back against him, rubbing her behind softly against the bulge at his zipper. "Great isn't it?"

"Dinner first, wench." He patted her fanny gently this time, "It was your idea, remember?"

Soon, they sat down and ate their dinner in companionable silence. The stereo was playing soft rock, and the dogs were locked outside. Several candles on the dining room table provided a soft, warm glow. Finally, sitting over the remains of the meal they began to talk again.

"I had a call from my mother today," Bob told her. "She complained about missing me at home. It seems she's been trying to reach me for several days."

"Do you even have a home?" Kate teased. "It seems like you're always here."

"I could leave." He started to rise.

"Not if you value your life," she threatened. "So what did

your mother want?"

"She's in her planning mode. She wants me to come to a family reunion, two weeks from Sunday," he informed her. "She wants you there, too."

"Where is this going to be?" Kate quizzed. "And how does she even know about me?"

"She knows I've been busy and not home, so she asked who it was and I described you." Bob gave a rueful laugh, "I think she likes you already, which is strange because she never liked my ex-wife, Jenna. I don't want to panic you, but I think she's been picking out names for our kids already."

"Hey, no panic. She can compare her list of names with my mother's, or Ida's," Kate laughed. "Ida wants me to stick with names beginning with the letter S."

"Anyway, it's supposed to be held at my folk's home in Reno." He noted her frown and put a finger over her mouth before she could even begin to voice her objections. "I have an alternative to the plan, however. I want to have it here, at my house. Both of my sisters, who happen to be one of the sets of the twins in my family, live nearby with their husbands and assorted kids. My brother, Jeff, and his family live in Arizona. If we have the reunion here, your family can come too. Your kids will be home by then. Heck, we can invite Ida, and even Charger can come."

"Do you have enough room?" Kate questioned. "I mean, your folks and your brother's family will have to stay over. Or did you plan to put them in a hotel?"

"I thought I'd give my brother and his family the house. He has the other set of twins, girls, so there's four of them." Bob smiled at Kate's expression, "I told you twins run in my family."

"You said run, but you never said they race." She moaned.

"My folks can stay with one of my sisters." Bob gave her a sly grin, "And I can stay here."

"There's one more to add to the list," Kate told him. "Since my mom's bringing the kids home so soon, my grandma's coming with her."

"When exactly are the kids coming home?" he questioned.

"Next Sunday," she sighed. "I'm enjoying my time alone and I still miss those guys like crazy."

"Isn't that sooner than you planned. What's up?" Bob was concerned.

"The kids are homesick. Mom misses dad. And grandma is coming with them because she wants to see me." She grinned at him, "Of course, they all want to get to know you. You are a curiosity, my dear. The first man I've dated since losing Joe."

"And I'd better be the last." He picked up his dishes and carried them into the kitchen, with Kate following. "Kate, you might want to consider postponing the kids' return until this is cleared up. The police think Jerry's unbalanced. That is, the ones who think I didn't kill him think he's unbalanced."

"I'll think about it." She hugged him, talking softly while leaning against his sweater, "I know it's silly but one of the reasons I want the kids home now, is so they can play with the puppies while they're so cute."

Bob gave her a reassuring squeeze, then went back to cleaning up the kitchen. He rinsed the dishes and put them into the dishwasher.

Finally he turned to Kate. "I thought we had plans for after dinner, wench."

"Yes Sir, oh lord and master sir." She bowed in front of him. "Shall I await your pleasure in the bedchamber or," she grinned, "just drop my drawers and climb on the kitchen table?"

He turned on the dishwasher and came over to stand in front of her. Gently and very slowly, his eyes intent on hers, he unbuttoned her silk blouse. He unfastened the front clasp of her lacy bra and slid the straps off her soft shoulders. She removed his tie, then reached up and unbuttoned his shirt, carefully removing his cuff links and putting them on the kitchen table.

She unbuckled his belt and unzipped his pants. He tugged her shorts gently down her long legs. She lowered his pants slowly down his legs. She was very careful and slow, gently working his underwear down his legs and passed the bulge of his manhood. He gave her a naughty grin and ripped the side of her panties in a quick motion.

"You . . . rat!" she sputtered.

"I'll buy you a dozen pair to replace them. I've always wanted to do that." He drank deeply of her mouth, "Let's go upstairs."

She took his hand and started up the stairs with him a step behind her, leaving the clothes strewn on the kitchen floor. Halfway up the stairs he stopped her by taking his free hand and reaching around to cup her breast, gently teasing at the nipple. Then he trailed his hand back around to her spine, and moved up to caress the back of her neck before moving slowly down again. She stood there, her back to him with one hand on the banister. Her other hand still held his; she felt a slight pull on it as he took a step back so that he was two steps below her.

She was startled and yet not surprised when she felt his lips and tongue kissing and teasing her spine and her rounded bottom. She gave a small jump when his teeth joined in the play, giving her a slight loving nip. He pulled his hand free from hers and used his hands on her hips to turn her gently around so that she faced him.

"Part your legs, love," he commanded, lowering his mouth to her moist femininity as she did so. He played with her, with his mouth, until her legs felt like they could no longer support her. She pulled slightly back and lay down on the carpeted steps. He joined her there, his mouth continuing its quest until he felt her stiffen against him and heard her gasping, throaty cry. He cuddled her in his arms, rolling over so that he was on the bottom, then she felt him laughing silently under her.

"Well, we probably can't do that again once the kids are

home," he said to her with a questioning glance.

"But there's still the bedroom." Standing up and pulling on his hand she continued, "You know the place we were headed before you got so distracted? Remember it has a big bed? We could go there now, and I could give you a little bit of payback."

"Well, I wouldn't want you to feel obligated, but if you insist." He stood up and lifted her, carrying her to the bed. "I guess I could let you even the score. Maybe we'll even start a whole new ball game after that."

"As long as you're not late for work tomorrow. I wouldn't want to make you late two mornings in a row." She lay back on the wide bed and reached for him.

"Then you'll just have to get me up early." He moaned as she trailed soft exploring kisses down his chest.

"No problem, I've got you up right now." She lowered her mouth to him.

Chapter Eleven

The next afternoon Kate was cleaning her house when she heard a knock at the front door. She found find a delivery boy on her front steps holding a large box. He handed her an envelope with a card in it.

The card said, *"Be sure to send the delivery boy away before you open this. Love, Bob."*

She gave the boy a generous tip, sending him on his way before she opened the box. There was a single, perfect red rose bud on top of the lilac tissue paper. Under the tissue paper was a couple of dozen pairs of soft, lacy panties and at least a dozen teddies, in all colors imaginable. Even a few lacy bras. As she explored her gift she found an envelope with something lumpy in it. She opened it to find a key and a note.

The note read: *I wish it was a key to my heart, but it's only the spare key to my house. Also, don't panic but my mother now has your phone number, and the reunion is definitely going to be at our house. I hope this makes up for the pair I ripped off your gorgeous, sexy body. I even bought extras in case some of these get "accidentally" torn, too. I love you. Bob.*

She called Bob at the office. "What a sappy, sentimental thing to do."

"You didn't like it?" he asked.

"I liked it so much it made me cry," she admitted.

"Women are weird, wonderful, but weird." He was laughing.

"Bob, one thing, you already gave me a key to your house. Remember the other night?" she asked softly.

"I remember that night very well. I know I told you to keep the key but I still want my neighbor to have a spare," he told her, leaning back in his office chair as he spoke to her, "and it seemed more romantic to give you a key than to give one to her. Symbolic somehow."

When he got home that evening, he was the only audience to a very short fashion show featuring female intimate apparel. However the planned show was cut short due to the audience's inability to keep his hands off the model.

They spent the weekend together quietly. A good portion of the time was really spent working. Bob brought home some of the paperwork that had been building up around the office while things were so unsettled. Shelly was in the hospital and Diana had moved into the now open cash room position, replacing Tonya. Diana was still able to keep up with the bank reconciliations even with her new cash room duties, but there were too many outstanding invoices piling up in Accounts Payable.

Bob and Kate worked online at her house. They entered data into a file and sent it to the office. They spent most of Friday evening posting invoices, then choosing and setting aside the bills that were due to be paid first.

They took a couple of short breaks from their work to eat dinner and play with the dogs. When they finally had the majority of the work brought up to date; they went upstairs to play in the shower before going to bed. On Saturday morning they actually decided to go into the office for a while. There was a ton of filing to do. They worked slowly, savoring the slightly naughty feeling of wearing T-shirts and shorts at work and fooling around in the office.

They also did a quick but careful search of Jerry's office. The unanswered questions were plaguing both of them. How did he know he was about to be caught? Did he know who had found the paper trail that led the police to him? Who were his accomplices? Where was he? Why had he needed the money? And, most important of all, was he bent on revenge or dangerous in any way? There were no answers to be found.

They ended the working morning on the sofa in Bob's office

making slow, passionate love, finally fulfilling a mutual but unspoken fantasy they had shared since she first walked into his office.

Finally, the conversation returned to work. "When Shelly is able to return to work, she'll take over Accounts Payable with a new girl, and you'll act as assistant controller, level with Laura. You'll focus more on Cost Accounting and Auditing. She'll cover Payables, Receivables and Bank Reconciliations. We'll need to hire the new girl right away to keep up the work in AP." Bob planned as they relaxed in his big, plush office.

"Is there enough work for you to have two assistant controllers?" Kate asked. "I mean, you've been doing just fine with one before now."

"True, but soon we'll be opening four more stores, taking over some of the regional work from Arizona, plus adding an in-house store credit card and a regional catalog sales office. The workload will go up quite a lot." Bob reminded her, "And Laura will have to cut back, sooner or later, because of her pregnancy. Our eventual forecast calls for four clerks handling AP and three handling Receivables, in addition to a new section dealing with credit and collections."

"So we hire?" she questioned.

"Yes, and we start now, so we have plenty of time to check references and do background checks. We want to have everyone in place and trained when the new stores open," he replied.

"Will you advertise or go through an agency?" She wanted to know.

"I thought I'd just leave it up to my new assistant controller," Bob whispered against her hair.

"Fine with me, but you realize that all the women I hire are going to be homely. Good, well-qualified workers, but homely," she threatened.

"That's okay, homely women need jobs, too. But is there really any such thing as a homely woman? I thought beauty was only skin deep," he kissed her, "that's what they say on all the talk shows."

"It is, and you're right." She kissed his nose lightly. "How politically correct of you, and I know you really mean it." Kate sighed, "But you can't blame me for trying, can you?"

"As long as the same code of appearance applies to the men you hire," he warned sternly.

"Of course not! I want handsome, well-built, single, muscular stud-muffins," she declared strongly. "I think Laura will back me up on this point, one hundred percent! Maybe we can go to the cove to recruit . . ."

Bob put a finger over her lips, "I have an idea, why don't we work together on the hiring? I'll pick the women and you pick the men?" Bob suggested.

"Or I could just drive you so crazy in bed that you won't even know what the female applicants look like," Kate teased.

"Now that sounds like a plan." Bob pushed her back into the deep cushions of the sofa again. "Kate, you aren't really jealous are you? Thinking that I might hire someone for their looks or make a play for them?"

"Of course not. You've never done it before me, and you sure won't now. Remember, trust is part of love? I'm just pulling your leg," she admitted.

"There's more of me for you to pull," he leered.

"Why boss man, how you talk." She pulled him down to her. "You'll have me blushing."

"As long as I have you, I don't care if you're blushing or not." He kissed her.

They spent early Saturday afternoon relaxing by Bob's pool before getting ready for Laura's party. Like most of the parties in Southern California at the hottest time of the year, it was to be a casual affair, a backyard barbecue with lots of hanging lanterns, loud music, and tables piled high with food. Unlike most parties, the main feature was a genuine pit barbecue.

Bob and Jack had dug the pit the day before and buried the meat. They used a corner of their backyard where a garden was soon going to be planted. Bob and Kate's relaxing afternoon was cut short when he had to go over to Laura's and help Jack dig up the beef. Kate went with him to see if she could help Laura with anything. Laura made a barbecue sauce from scratch that made Kate's head swim, but it was really terrific, and the meat was perfect, tender, juicy and had a great smoky flavor.

Once the food was ready they went home to dress up for the casual party. Kate fussed over her appearance, something Bob claimed must be a woman's thing. He was happy as long as he could grab a quick shower and put on clean denim shorts and a polo shirt. Kate, however, had more to do than shower and change into a party dress. She washed her hair and dried it, then she brushed her hair, used her curling iron to give it some body, and piled it on top of her head. Then she started putting on make-up.

"What exactly is the difference between dressing up for a casual party and dressing up for a formal one?" Bob asked as he watched her, fascinated.

"When you dress up for a casual party, you use a tad less make-up, do your hair yourself, and wear a dress that's perfect but casual," Kate explained. "For a formal affair, you have your hair and nails done, use more dramatic make-up and buy a dress that's to die for."

"Makes sense to me." Bob grinned indulgently, "Are you going to wear my favorite sundress?"

"If you'd like." she laughed at him. "I do have other dresses, you know."

"But I like the way that one shows off your, um . . . assets."

"Pig." She grinned, reaching for the dress.

At the party, aside from the two of them and Laura and Jack, there was quite an expected guest list: Frank and John, some of Jack and Laura's friends, and almost everyone from the office accounting department, and their dates or spouses, even a few of their kids. Laura even invited most of the neighborhood so that they wouldn't call the cops if it got too noisy.

Shortly before leaving to go to Laura's, Bob told Kate, "All the women from the office will be there. John approved it because they've all been completely cleared. I held a short meeting and told them you were investigating the thefts. They understand that you were only dismissed as a ploy to make the real thief relax and show himself or herself. What they don't know is that you were involved in catching Tonya. All I told them was about your investigation of Jerry's embezzling."

"Do they see me as a snitch?" She put down her mascara and turned away from the mirror to face him, worried.

"No, most of them realized that their jobs were at stake and you saved those jobs." He grinned and kissed her before handing the lipstick to her. "At least that's how I told it."

"But there is some resentment?" she asked with concern still in her eyes.

"Rita and Mary are a little upset because they stood up for you when you didn't need it." He told her, "Remember, both of them went after me at one time or another. Laura too."

"I'll have to smooth some ruffled feathers," she smiled a bit sadly, "and thank them; I really appreciated their support and sympathy even if it wasn't totally necessary."

"If you give me a romantic kiss me in front of them it may go a long, long way towards soothing those feelings. Both of them have been trying to get me fixed up with someone as long as I've known them." Bob suggested, "Give them credit for playing cupid."

"No problem, I'll give you a romantic kiss wherever you'd like, and as often as you'd like. Maybe I'll enlist the two of them in our plan to get Cheryl and John together. Then, of course, Laura and I have to go to work on Frank." She smiled. "I promised to find him a shrew."

"A shrew?" Bob was puzzled. "Why do you want to find him a shrew?"

"So I can watch her tame him, of course, it should be a wonderful match." She sighed dreamily, "He'll run and fight. There should be some wild and interesting battles, but if we find the right woman, he'll lose, big time."

"I thought you were his friend." Bob was still trying to figure it out.

"Bob, my love, get a move on, we'll be late." As they went to the door, she explained, "In the case of love, if he loses the fight, he'll really win the war. You'd better understand that, darling, or you're in big hairy trouble."

"Yes dear. I'm glad you're here to straighten me out." Bob faked a sheepish expression.

"Darn right, Bozo, my love." She kissed him before she got into the car, reaching down to give him a friendly pat on the zippered front of his slacks. "And parts of you straighten out really well."

"I'm glad you think so." He went around and got into the driver's side. "How long do we have to stay at this party anyway?"

"Not long, just until John has caught Cheryl's interest, the accounting staff is back to their usual happy selves, and Laura and I have formulated a plan to get Petruchio, I mean Frank, a shrew." She smiled and snapped her fingers. "We should be home and asleep by midnight."

"Correction Kate, we'll be in bed by midnight. Sleep will take a little longer." Bob smiled in anticipation.

When they arrived at the party, most of the office staff came over to greet them. Frank caught her in a big hug, all the while grinning defiantly at Bob. He released her, kissing her cheek and she turned away to be greeted by the others.

Cheryl gave her a quick hug. "I can't tell you how glad I am that you're going to be coming back."

Rita was the next closest staff member, but she made no move over to Kate, so Kate walked over to her and hugged her.

"Rita, I have to thank you for being my friend and comforter, even though I really wasn't in any trouble." Kate said softly, "Will you forgive me for deceiving you?"

"Sure. I'm just glad to know that Laura and Bob aren't really turning into slave drivers," Rita said in a grudging manner.

"Oh, Bob's okay. He helped Laura with the cost of the food. Besides, I think he's kinda cute." Kate's eyes flashed. "Do you think I should make a play for him?"

"I think you probably already did." Rita looked at her shrewdly.

"Darn right, I'm not dumb. So who's this handsome man?" She turned to Rita's escort, a short man of about sixty with an interesting, but homely face.

"That's Fred, my husband. After thirty years, I guess I'm stuck with him." Kate and Fred shook hands.

Kate turned to give Mary a hug. "Thank you so much for being my defender. I hear you told Laura off in no uncertain terms. I hope you realize now that she was just playing a part, she's been my best friend for more years than I want to even think about." She was introduced to Mary's husband, a tall good-looking Hispanic man. She also turned to greet Jennifer, Diana and Sherry and their boyfriends. Hugging each woman briefly and talking to each one individually, she made peace with them all.

Sherry drew her away from the group. "Did you have anything to do with Tonya being fired?" she asked Kate pointedly.

"Yes, I'm afraid I did. I'm sorry but I found out there was money being stolen by someone in the cash room. I didn't know which one of you was behind it, so I left it to Bob and John from Loss Prevention." Kate paused. "They both went out of their way to make sure you were never falsely accused or made to feel like you were under suspicion. They didn't want you to be uncomfortable. They really care about your feelings."

"I see." Sherry smiled weakly, "I have to think about that awhile. I guess you had no choice once you found the problem, you had to report it. I'll admit I was feeling betrayed, like they were spying on me, but it would have been worse to be accused and questioned. Thank you for explaining that."

Kate left the women and went in search of Bob. She took the wineglass out of his hand and sipped it before handing it back to him. Then she reached up and pulled his mouth down to hers, kissing him firmly and possessively on the mouth.

"I don't think the natives are restless anymore," she told him, "and I'm going to party. How many glasses of wine have you had?"

"This is my first, why?" he wondered.

"You are hereby designated to be the sober driver, that was your last glass of wine," she told him firmly.

"Yes, Ma'am. But can I still dance?" he asked dutifully.

"Of course, but you are only allowed to enjoy it when you're dancing with me." Kate saw the door opening. "Oh good. Here's John."

She went over to greet him and led him over to the buffet table where Cheryl was filling her plate.

"John, here's the food, help yourself." She smiled. "Oh! Have you met Cheryl?"

"Pleased to meet you." He smiled at Cheryl, holding out his hand.

"It's nice to meet you too." She watched as Kate walked away. "Something seemed funny about that introduction. It seemed sort of pointed. What was it? Do you think she made a point of introducing us because we're the only African Americans here? Or am I nuts?"

"Let's sit over there," he said, pointing to a bench at the side of the yard, "and I'll tell you about it."

They walked over and sat down, their plates balanced carefully on their laps. "So, what's up?" Cheryl asked.

"I hope this doesn't upset you but Kate made a point of introducing us because I asked about you when I saw you at the office, and she thought I wanted to get to know you," John admitted.

He smiled and continued, "In fact, Laura planned this party about three seconds after Kate shared that bit of information with her. They're matchmaking and that short, pointed introduction was the reason why Laura threw this party."

"I knew Laura was ruthless, but Kate too?" Cheryl gulped her drink down. She studied John's face for a minute, noting his warm humor and quick intelligence. It also didn't hurt that he was handsome and well dressed in a white polo shirt and black pants. Not bad, she thought to herself.

She smiled, "Well in that case you'd better at least dance with me since this kind of effort should be rewarded."

"Or else Laura will drag you down to the nude beach," John agreed. At Cheryl's questioning gaze he told her what he knew about how Bob and Kate really met.

"Well, face it John, we may have met our fate," Cheryl teased.

"It's too soon to be sure," John remarked. "But maybe."

"Do you know how many married couples I know that met through Laura?" Cheryl asked with a touch of desperation in her voice.

"How many?" John looked into her pretty eyes and smiled.

"Tons," Cheryl said, "and I've never seen her miss yet."

"Then to quote the old song, let's face the music and dance." John laughed.

He took her drink and set it on a table, then he led her to the dance floor. Just as he took her into his arms, he whispered in her ear, "It may be fate, but it's such a *good* fate."

Neither John nor Cheryl noticed as Laura and Kate exchanged high fives on the other side of the room. Bob and Jack came over to join them.

"Who are you two going to plot against next?" Jack asked them.

"Frank," Kate answered instantly.

"I should have seen that one coming," Jack muttered.

"Who do we know that's special enough?" Laura asked.

"And spirited enough," Kate added. "I promised Frank a shrew that would give him a hard time and put him in his place."

"That leaves out my choice, Emily. She's too sweet and gentle. I wish I could find someone special for her, I don't know anyone who needs or deserves to be loved more," Laura sighed.

"I've met Emily," Kate reminded her. "She is very sweet and she does deserve someone special, but not Frank, she's too gentle for him."

"And you're right, Frank needs a spirited woman who can stand toe to toe with him," Laura admitted.

"Who do you think he would go for then?" Kate thought aloud.

Both women looked up as they heard a shriek coming from the side of the yard where the bar was set up. They looked up to see Frank get slapped and then yelled at by a short, slender, redheaded wildcat.

"You great lumbering oaf! Why the heck don't you use those big brown eyes if you plan to walk around with a full drink in your hand? It would have to be a bloody Mary!" the woman fumed.

"You ran into me you little danger zone, I was standing still." Frank was so much taller than the unknown woman that he had to lean over to yell in her face. He bent down until he was almost nose to nose with his combative new acquaintance.

"Who's that?" Kate narrowed her eyes, speculating.

"Lanie McPherson. She's a friend of Jack's from work," Laura said. "She's single and has a daughter. Jack told me that she got a hard time from some of the other landscape architects at the office when she was first hired. She's tough enough that she fought back in her own way."

"What did she do?" Kate asked.

"She worked hard enough and long enough to buy in as a partner. Then she made sure better sexual harassment policies were put in place." Laura smiled. "Still, she left room for innocent banter and fun between co-workers."

"She looks perfect to me," Kate said, listening to her haranguing Frank. "Man! She's got a fiery temper."

"And they met without our interference," Laura said. "He can't even blame us."

"She'll give him a hard time," Kate said softly. "A real hard time."

They looked at each other and said in unison, "Perfect!"

Bob and Jack exchanged long-suffering sighs. "Another one bites the dust," Bob said.

"Poor fool's going to go down fighting," Jack replied. "He won't give in without a fight like you did."

"I know Laura too well, I decided to go to my fate bravely, like a man," Bob said, then he caught Kate giving him a look, her eyebrows raised. "Of course, I couldn't fight because I fell in love at first glance. What a sight that was."

"My first glance was pretty impressive too." Kate kissed him.

"Let's go break up the fight and see if we can rescue her dress. It would have to be white linen." Laura sighed. "Such a beautiful dress, too. It really is a shame."

She and Kate went over and interrupted the fight, separating the combatants. Laura took Lanie upstairs and loaned her a dress, a very sexy sundress, and gently blotted up as much of the stain as she could off the linen dress.

Downstairs Kate had Frank cornered, literally, next to the tiny dance floor. "So? Do you think you could tame that shrew?"

"Piece of cake, but why would I want to?" Frank asked.

"She's very smart and good-looking. And she knows how to

stand up for herself," Kate listed her qualities. "But you couldn't handle her, I'd bet on it."

"What do you mean you'd bet on it?" Frank seemed insulted.

"Well, it would be a bet I couldn't lose." Kate eyed him speculatively. "You'd never get the girl."

"I could if I wanted too," Frank defied her.

"When that happens I'll have you right where I want you, married to her. Unsettled, upset and never bored, but very, very happy." Kate held out her hand. "Bet?"

"Bet," Frank said, clasping her hand and feeling trapped. He tried one last ploy. "Unless I could bet against myself?"

"No way. You already shook hands on it." She laughed and looked around for Bob. "You're done for and my work here is done. I'm gonna grab my old man and blow this pop stand."

She walked over to where Bob and Jack were talking in the corner. "Hi sailor, new in town?"

"I'm just looking for the right woman to take me home and put me to bed," Bob told her. "Is Frank all taken care of?"

"He's finished. I backed him into a bet." She paused before she explained, "I bet him that he couldn't get her to marry him within a year, and he bet he could."

"He took that bet?" Bob said incredulously. "I don't even want to know how you managed that."

"I double dared him." She grinned.

"Bob, we have got to keep our two women apart. The fate of the free world could be at stake." Jack shook his head laughing, "And I thought Laura was scary all by herself."

"Well I have to tell Laura the terms of the bet so she can help me lose," Kate said, "then we can leave. By the way, how *is* John doing with Cheryl?"

"Sparks are flying, it looks like we have a winner," Bob told her. "John kissed her on the dance floor."

"I'd like it better if he kissed her on the mouth," she joked. "I'll be right back." She went over and had a short conference with Laura. When she returned, she took Bob by the hand and tried to lead him out the door.

"Hey wait!" Bob protested, then his voice dropped. "I'm glad you want to go home and be alone with me. I want to be with you, too. But this is a party and there's a whole side of beef that I helped cook, and some of it has my name on it. Plus, there are salads and side dishes and about four different cakes I'd like to sample. Can't we eat here? Unless you'd like to cook at home."

"Okay, we'll stay for dinner. Since you cooked," she laughed, "with your trusty shovel. But you only get to sample three cakes, not all four. I don't want you to get fat." She kissed him, rubbing his flat, washboard stomach. "On the other hand, sample all the cakes if you want. We'll work it off at home."

They relaxed and enjoyed themselves, eating and dancing and visiting with their friends, but not for very long. There was a bed waiting for them.

Chapter Twelve

It was nearly midnight when Kate and Bob finally left the party and headed for her house. They were feeling slightly tired but still amorous and wickedly happy. However those feelings ceased as soon as Kate opened her front door. She knew immediately something was wrong.

Very, very wrong.

Teddy and Charger didn't come charging to the door to greet her. She got a glimpse of the living room. It was in a total shambles. Kate froze, one hand on the doorknob. Bob also realized something was terribly wrong inside the house. Her next reaction was to check on her beloved animals but Bob's good sense prevailed. He grabbed her by the shoulders.

"We can't do anything here. I know you want to go in and so do I, but we would only mess up any clues for the police." He restrained her gently, "Let's go call them from my car."

They went back to Bob's car and got in. Bob used his cell phone to call the police and report that Kate's house had been broken into.

Kate was shaking. "God! I hope they didn't hurt Teddy or Charger. I'm so scared. They always run to the door to greet me." Then another thought hit her, adding to her fear. "Bob, no one would hurt the puppies, would they? No one could be that cruel, that sick."

She started to open the car door, planning on going in the house to check on the dogs but Bob stopped her. He cuddled her close to his chest, soothing and calming her even though he was very scared and angry himself. He kept telling himself it was only a burglar or kids on drugs, but he knew who had broken into

Kate's house. He was filled with nervous tension and blind fury. In his mind he kept hearing the warning from the police that Jerry could be dangerous, even unbalanced.

When the police arrived, Bob got out of the car to talk to them, leaving a shaky Kate in the car. He told them that no one had left the house while they were there, at least not from the front. Then he told them about the dogs and the puppies, explaining that Kate was frantic to go in and see if they were all right. One of the police officers entered the house; soon he came out again carrying the squealing litter in its box. The puppies were fine.

"If the barking coming out of the downstairs bathroom is anything to go by, I'd say the parents of these little critters are all right, too. They sounded really ferocious. I decided I wasn't going to be the one to open that door," the officer stated, grinning ruefully. "Even if they *are* small dogs."

Kate got out of the car and went in the house, consciously shutting out the wreckage in her living room. She let the two dogs out of the bathroom. Then she quickly put them on their leashes and took them outside.

"Can you tell if anything is missing Ma'am?" one of the officers asked after she put the dogs in Bob's car.

She went back into the house and walked through it carefully. This time she had to let all the damage sink in and it was devastating. Bob was beside her all the way, holding her arm as she checked over the house and looked at her possessions.

Everything was either smashed, torn or overturned, but everything seemed to be there. Her TV and VCR were smashed and her computer monitor was broken. The computer's tower was gone and her back-up discs were also missing. She pointed that out to the police.

She went upstairs and found out that the destruction was just as bad up there. Her comforter and pillows were slashed, along with her mattress. Most of her clothes were ripped, even her new lingerie. Sadly, even the kids' rooms hadn't escaped the destruction. There were torn clothes and broken toys spread all over the floor.

There was only one loss that really devastated her, one blow that seemed to defeat her totally. She found her wedding photo album and all of her family photo albums, ruined. Those albums had all of her pictures of Joe and the baby pictures of her kids. The precious pictures were all torn to shreds or covered with something black and sticky. The sight of it stopped her in her tracks. She sank to her knees in tears.

Bob was shocked at the wanton destruction and also angry, angrier than he had ever been in his life at the useless and cruel destruction of all of her irreplaceable pictures. He was shocked at himself to realize that there was also a strangely disturbing undercurrent to his sympathy.

This was the first time he had really faced exactly what the loss of her husband had meant to Kate, and how much she had loved him. It disturbed him a bit. It wasn't exactly jealousy. It was the realization that he could share his life with her and the kids, but he could never be the one she planned to have those kids with. The one she had planned to grow old with. He could love them and maybe be a father to them but it was important to Kate that the kids always remember Joe, who had loved them and fathered them first.

Once he realized that, he knew that was the way it should be. Joe deserved his place in Kate's and the kids' lives. He would have to carve his own place alongside Joe's, without replacing him. He gently helped Kate over to the sofa and sat with her, holding her and trying in vain to comfort her. Gradually she came back to some semblance of control and she began to be aware of her surroundings once more.

She realized that along with her computer's tower and the discs, the files she had brought from work were gone. They were not on the floor around where her overturned, smashed coffee table used to be.

For Kate and Bob that was all the proof they needed; Jerry had done this. Without words, they both thought about how dangerous and unbalanced Jerry must have become. Why would he do these things? For that matter, why had he stolen so much money in the first place?

The senior patrol officer gestured for Bob to come over and talk to him. He left Kate on the sofa and walked over to the policeman.

"What threw her into such a tailspin?" he asked Bob curiously. "She was holding up fairly well until she found the mess in the den."

"Kate was widowed when her children were very young, hell, the oldest is not yet five now," Bob explained. "The bastard who did this tore up all the pictures she had of her husband, including her wedding pictures and the pictures of him with the kids. She almost feels like she lost him again."

"You haven't been together very long then?" he quizzed. "You seem like an established couple."

"No. Sometimes love hits you like that, I guess. I was lost the first time we met," Bob told the officer.

"This has to be a grudge. Do you realize, really realize, how sick and dangerous this man is?" the officer queried.

Bob looked at the patrolman. "I have more to tell you about this but let me get Kate out of here for now. I can put her in my car."

Bob went back to Kate and led her outside. He put her into his car before he went over and talked to the officers, telling them about the thefts at work and her investigation. One of the patrolmen took the name of the officer handling that case to add to his report, and promised to contact that officer about this break-in. Bob also gave him the name and address of their suspect, Jerry Weisner.

At the patrol officer's request, Kate reluctantly knocked on her neighbor Tim's door. He came out in a bathrobe and for once in his grubby life, was surprisingly cooperative, answering the patrolman's questions. He even described a car he had seen at the house earlier that night. It matched the description of Jerry's car, a blue Honda Civic. He said it was there when they left for the party.

"I'm sorry I didn't call the cops then, doll, but I thought maybe lover boy just had a new car until I saw you leave for the party with him. Then I just forgot about it," he told Kate. "Hey, is it serious with him?"

"Yes, it is, Tim." She gave him a faint, trembling smile. "I hope you're happy for me."

"Well he's more suited for a classy dame like you than I am, but you make him treat you right," he told her before asking, "Want a beer?"

"Do you have any whiskey?" Kate told him, "I think I'm way past beer right now."

He went in his house and brought out a shot of bourbon for her. Kate downed it in a single gulp.

She looked up at Tim and said, "Thanks, I needed that."

Tim grinned, "See? I knew you had class."

Kate went back to join Bob, vaguely wondering what downing a shot of good bourbon had to do with class, but glad she seemed to have made peace with her neighbor at last.

It seemed like forever but finally, they were finished dealing with the police. It was after two AM. Wearily, they got into Bob's car and made the short drive over to his place, dogs and all.

During the drive, Kate came out of her initial shock enough to realize fully just how dangerous a person Jerry really was. She glanced over at Bob as he drove and noticed the tightness of his face, and how white his knuckles were as they gripped the steering wheel; she knew he had come to the same conclusion.

As they pulled into Bob's driveway, they saw a car driving very fast down the street towards the freeway. Since it was so dark, they couldn't determine the make or color but for some reason both of them found the car disturbing. It seemed familiar somehow.

They got out of Bob's car and headed for the house. Bob was carrying the box full of puppies and Kate was holding Teddy and Charger on their leashes. She used her new key to open his door and then gasped as she saw the mess in his living room.

Stunned and shaken beyond belief, they went back to Bob's car and called the police again. This time, they followed that call with calls to Laura and to John.

The car was simply too confining for their emotions, so they got out. Both of them were feeling so blazingly furious and agitated that it almost sickened them. While waiting for the police, they sat on the lawn feeling like victims of a very bad joke. Every once in a while one of them would get up and pace around the small lawn.

Bob had told the operator answering the police phone about the break-in at Kate's and gave them the name of the patrol officer he had spoken to earlier. The same officer was between calls so he was first to arrive on the scene.

"This is like a bad movie," Bob said, shaking the man's hand.

"We've got to stop meeting like this," Kate greeted him, quipping bravely but with a trembling voice.

"No critters inside the house this time, we brought them with us." Bob told the officer about the car that they had seen driving away. "And I called the head of security for our business; he's been working with the detectives on the embezzlement case. Plus I called my assistant at work, just in case she's a target, too," Bob told the patrolman. "She was involved in the investigation at work."

"Good thinking. I'll need those names," the officer said. "I called the detectives who were working the embezzlement case and told them of the first break-in. In fact, they're at your house, Ma'am, conducting a follow-up investigation. I'll call them again right now."

Bob walked through the house, just as Kate had walked through hers earlier. As in the case with Kate's house, destruction not theft, seemed to be the motive. This time, although there was clearly less damage than at Kate's house the total effect was a clear picture of madness. Bob's house was, in essence, only damaged downstairs. Upstairs only his mattress and the sheets on his bed were slashed. His clothes were scattered on the floor but not torn apart.

It was almost as if he had been interrupted before he had a chance to destroy everything upstairs. Downstairs, all of the small appliances in the kitchen were broken, his television and VCR were ruined, and all of his furniture had been slashed and smashed. Once again, the tower was gone from his computer, and any files he'd brought home had been taken.

About an hour later, Kate and Bob sat in his living room talking to John. He seemed tired as he sat there gently stroking his puppy. He went over the evening's events with them. They told him everything they could about both break-ins. John spoke with the police about the situation at work.

Finally, the police told Bob and Kate they could leave. One of the officers got a phone number and address from Kate for where they expected to be for the next few days. It was almost five AM when it was decided that Kate and Bob would spend the rest of the night with her dad at her parents' house. They would have gone to a motel, but with six dogs that didn't seem even remotely possible. On Sunday, John, Laura, Jack and maybe even Cheryl would help them clean up their houses.

"Let's meet at Kate's first thing in the morning and work on the clean up there, then we can finish at my house," Bob suggested. "We'll grill some steaks and try to relax when we get done cleaning up."

"Okay, but I think we should wait until Monday," John suggested. "You and Kate need to unwind, and it'll give me time to organize a clean-up crew and get some dumpsters at both houses."

"Okay, thanks John." Bob walked him to the door and shook his hand.

John discreetly pulled Bob outside; he and Bob briefly discussed how they could use the company's security force to protect Kate without being too obvious. They also wanted to coach Kate on some basic self-defense. It wasn't a case of using Kate as bait to trap Jerry as much as being ready to catch him when and if he made his move. Whether or not they surrounded her with security, anyone as sick as Jerry was bound to try something sooner or later. Both men knew it, and Kate knew it too.

Kate and Bob found her parents' house empty. She used her spare key to let them in. Evidently her father had taken advantage of his time alone, since a quick search revealed his tackle box and favorite fishing pole were gone.

"If past history is anything to go by," Kate told Bob, "he's in a cabin up at Lake Tahoe." Kate wondered aloud if he was really fishing or if he was spending most of his time at the casinos in Reno.

"I can't help but be a little relieved that he's gone," Bob told her. "I really want to meet your dad but not by showing up at his house after five in the morning with his daughter and six dogs asking for a place to sleep."

"Especially since I told you he's already decided to give you a hard time about fooling around with me. Of course, you'll also get the third degree about your health, education, job, marriage, and financial status." Kate pulled him into the kitchen. "Come on, let's raid the fridge."

They soon learned that her dad had cleaned out the refrigerator and left it empty except for one lonely frozen pizza. They decided to leave it; they weren't really hungry, just edgy. They curled up in Kate's old bedroom and tried to sleep. They were both upset and they didn't have any clean clothes to wear in the morning but at least the bed had clean sheets, the house wasn't torn apart, the phone lines weren't cut, and they were safe.

Considering the time they got to bed, they awoke early the next morning cuddled in each other's arms. It was only eight AM. Something woke them up. It took a moment for them to realize exactly what had awakened them. The sound of the front door opening and closing, and her dogs scampering and barking. Kate's father had come home.

Kate bounded out of the bed and pulled her dress over her head.

She went downstairs quickly, pausing only long enough to warn Bob, "Hurry up and get dressed. You'd better get downstairs before he comes looking for you."

"Daddy!" Kate hugged her father. "Boy, am I glad to see you."

"What happened, Sweetheart? Did that new man give you trouble? I love having you here, but what's up?" Her father was concerned by the wounded look in her eyes.

"No, Daddy, it's nothing like that. Bob would never hurt me. There's been someone embezzling at our office and I found the proof that incriminated the thief," Kate told her father with pride in her voice. "He disappeared and the cops can't find him. Last night he vandalized my house, partly trying to see if I had any evidence on him and partly for revenge." Her voice caught as her composure broke. "Daddy, he tore up everything I own, he destroyed all my pictures of Joe."

Bob came over to join them, sliding his arms around Kate's waist and extending one hand to Kate's father. "Hi, I'm Bob. We went to my house and found out that he had torn it apart, too. So we needed someplace safe to spend the night, at least, what was left of it after the police were finished with us. I hope you don't mind us coming over like this, but we had to find a place to stay where we could bring the dogs."

"Were you fooling around with my daughter in my own house?" Kate's father narrowed his eyes at Bob.

"Sir, last night was a time for support and comfort. It was not a time for anything else." Bob met his gaze steadily.

"But you do sleep with her whenever you can?" her father asked Bob sternly.

"Daddy!" Kate shrieked.

Bob met the older man's eyes with a steady gaze. "Yes sir, I do. I love her."

"It's about time she found someone to love," her father said curtly. "Kate, go fix us breakfast, I want to talk to Bob here alone."

Bob turned to Kate who was opening her mouth to protest and said, "Go on, love. It's a father's greatest joy to give his daughter's man a hard time. You wouldn't want to deprive him of that now, would you?"

Kate found a shopping bag filled with food on the kitchen counter. Evidently her father stopped and stocked up before coming home. Kate made pancakes, eggs, and bacon, plus a pot of fresh, strong coffee. By the time Kate had breakfast on the table, the two men seemed to be as thick as thieves. They each had a shot of her father's best whiskey in front of them, before breakfast no less! They looked up at Kate and suddenly both of them broke out laughing.

"Men!" Kate put her hands on her hips and shook her head. She reached out and took Bob's drink, swallowing it in one gulp. "Breakfast is ready."

After breakfast, Kate and Bob went shopping for some new clothes and personal items. Monday morning, they met with their friends at Kate's house. Kate's father, who had driven all Saturday night and spent Sunday talking with Kate and Bob, crashed. He decided he needed to get some more sleep before joining the work party but would come over later.

Laura brought her video camera and John brought a still

camera. The first thing they did was document all the damage for the insurance companies, with both videotape and still photographs. Bob contacted both of their agents. Bob also arranged to have the cut phone lines repaired at both houses. He also called a security company that John had recommended, to get burglar alarms installed at both houses.

Cheryl arrived a little later than everyone else. She joined the group, jumping in on the cleaning and straightening process. Then Jack drove up with one of the large panel trucks his landscaping firm owned. They filled a dumpster to the brim at Kate's house and loaded all the rest of the broken and ruined items onto the truck. Then they arranged and straightened anything that was worth saving, which was precious little, and cleaned up as well as possible. The destruction was so complete that the only piece of furniture left intact downstairs at Kate's house was a floor lamp her parents had given her years before. Kate had always privately thought it was the ugliest thing she had in the house.

Kate's dad saw it and said, "Look honey, the lamp's not broken." He grinned at Kate. "Isn't that great?"

"Great, Daddy." She tried to smile.

"Of course, it is the ugliest thing I've ever seen. Maybe now is a good time to throw it out," her father said.

"Daddy! You know that lamp is hideously ugly?" Kate was astonished.

"Of course I do. Your mother only bought it because she was mad at me. Why do you think we gave it to you?" he teased her.

"Gee, thanks Dad," Kate grinned slyly, "and all this time I thought you loved me." She smiled widely. "Let's give it to the Salvation Army."

"With your luck, you'll find out someday that it's a valuable collector's item," her father teased.

"A trash collector's item," she agreed.

After finishing at Kate's house, the whole group went over to Bob's house to repeat the clean-up process; Jack made a detour to the dump before joining them at Bob's. It turned out that the destruction was not nearly so complete at Bob's. His sofa and chairs in the den could be salvaged, but they would need to be recovered. His television, VCR, and stereo were completely ruined, but his collection of videotapes and CDs were for the most part, intact.

Upstairs, his bedroom was torn apart, his mattress and bedspread slashed to shreds, but his clothes were mainly undamaged. They had been thrown on the floor and some of the shirts were ripped but the rest of his wardrobe was only wrinkled.

Once they had things under control at Bob's, Laura and Kate left for a while. They bought some steaks, beer, and wine while the men started the barbecue. Kate's dad went home and brought over the dogs.

Everybody appeared to relax, but it was only on the surface. No one could forget the total and wanton devastation they had just cleaned up. They tried to enjoy their meals. It was a beautiful evening, and after dinner everyone jumped in the pool.

Laura and Jack didn't stay long; they went for a short swim and then left. Cheryl and John seemed to be growing steadily closer but it wasn't the instant passion that had hit Bob and Kate. They stayed for a while but not too long, seeming to realize that Kate and Bob wanted to be alone to regroup.

Once everyone was gone Kate and Bob settled together on a chaise lounge, holding each other and talking about the break-ins, work, and especially Jerry. Somehow, in spite of the hard work and genuine worry of the day, things gradually got more and more romantic. Kate felt Bob's lips moving softly, nuzzling her ear and her hair.

"Kate," he said, "I have an idea. It may seem like it just occurred to me because of all that's happened, but it didn't. It just seems like this is perfect timing. I mean. . ."

"What is it?" Kate prodded, "So far you've done everything but tell me whatever it is you're trying to tell me."

"I know I wasn't making sense. Here's my idea." Bob hesitated. "Why don't you stay with me until Jerry's caught and we have the family reunion? We can live here together and fix up my house first, then worry about yours. So don't start replacing all that stuff that got destroyed just yet, just get the essentials and wait a while for everything else, okay?"

"I can't buy much before the insurance company comes through anyway," she told him. "I don't have as large an emergency fund as you probably do."

"There's more behind this than that. I don't want to tell you just yet though, for the time being just trust me, please love?" He pulled her into his arms and she forgot all about his mysterious request. "By the way, the reunion's been postponed indefinitely, until after Jerry is caught."

"What about my kids? They're coming home next Sunday," she worried.

"Remember I said it might be a wise idea for them to stay at your grandmother's until Jerry is caught?" He pointed out, "I think you'd better consider it."

"You're right, I can't bring them home while Jerry is out there. But what then?" she wondered.

"They can stay here too, unless you feel awkward about moving them in here with me," he told her. "I mean, if you feel like it's not right somehow."

"When Jerry's been arrested and he's out of the picture, we'll face the question of my moving in with you. I should have known it would happen someday," she paused, choosing her words, "being a single parent, I mean. It makes things like living together even more important. I have to have a normal life, and I'm an adult. I don't think it will do any harm for them to see me happy and in love." She gave him an impish smile. "The person who's going to make things really awkward is my father. Dad will lecture you about messing around with his little girl."

"Your dad already knows about it." He kissed her soundly.

"That's why he brought over the dogs, he knows you're here to stay. You're not going anywhere."

The next day they went back to work in the office. The whole embezzling scheme had been fully outlined; it turned out that Jerry only had one accomplice in the plan, and he was more of a dupe than a real accomplice.

He was just a kid working in the receiving department. He didn't even know for sure what Jerry was really doing, or that it was illegal. He was more than willing to testify against Jerry when he learned how close he came to being fired and arrested as an accomplice.

Jerry was the only suspect and everyone else was in the clear. Because Jerry had not been arrested, Kate felt better at work with Bob than being home by herself. That was part of why Kate went back to work at the office. Also, as pragmatic as it was, there was still work to get done.

There was a whole different feeling to the office. Seeing Bob and Kate working together, the last traces of resentment held by the other clerks faded. For their part, Bob and Kate just enjoyed being themselves. They weren't exhibitionists, no one saw them kissing in the hallway like teenagers, but their affection for each other showed every time they were together. Even though they were both afraid and waiting for the other shoe to drop, their joy and happiness was contagious, raising the spirits and protective instincts of their co-workers.

They were both still conscious that the police had failed to catch Jerry, so they couldn't relax. In spite of the damage he did to their houses, both Kate and Bob tried to convince themselves that Jerry had gotten his revenge and fled. On the outside, they appeared to get back to a normal routine.

Each evening, Kate helped Bob shop and pick out things as he refurbished his house. Monday night they started with the master bedroom. Bob called the store from work and arranged to have a new mattress delivered. After work, Kate helped him pick out new pillows, sheets, and a velour comforter, along with a lamp and a new clock radio. She decided to throw out his old area rugs and redecorate the room in shades of rich burgundy.

The only things they hurried to replace downstairs were the television, VCR, and stereo. For some reason, they never spent much time in the large family room anyway. After a full day's work and shopping for the new furnishings they needed, they stopped off for fast food then went home and jumped in the pool for a late swim before going straight to bed. They were almost too tired to make love, almost.

By the end of the first week they had Bob's bedroom, kitchen and den refurnished, and they had decorated his two spare bedrooms for the kids. Kate debated with Bob over that, insisting that since they were only staying with him until her own place was fixed up it was too much trouble, but he was adamant about it.

The very idea that he wanted to make his home comfortable for her kids to live in gave her a deep reservoir of hope. They hadn't known each other very long but Kate knew exactly what she wanted. She had known almost from the moment she looked up at Bob on the beach. It wasn't because of his looks or his very impressive body. There was something more in his eyes or his voice that had caught her attention and told her he was the one.

Kate believed Bob felt the same way, but she wasn't sure. Bob told her that he loved her but so far he never once mentioned marriage. Still, she took heart from the rooms decorated especially for her kids. He did one more thing that made her think his plans were permanent. It was just a little thing but it gave her hope.

He installed a doggie door.

Chapter Thirteen

The next Friday Bob left work soon after lunch. He told everyone in the office that he had some very special errands to run and there was a secretive gleam in his eye, but he refused to tell anyone about it. Kate wanted to come with him, but her nose was really put out of joint when he told her to get back to work. She took this with her usual grace and charm; she stuck her tongue out at him behind his back. She was so tied up in her work for the rest of the day that she was buried under an avalanche of papers at quitting time.

"Aren't you going home?" she heard Laura ask.

Kate looked up, startled. "Is it that time? I still have a mess piled up here. I won't be long. I only have about thirty minutes of work left on these accounts, then I should straighten up my desk and leave."

"Do you want me to stay with you?" Laura asked with concern in her voice. "Remember, they haven't caught Jerry yet. You shouldn't be here alone, it's not safe."

"No, go home, I'll be fine. There are plenty of security guards around." Kate grinned. "You know Bob and John have got me covered."

It didn't take long for her to finish her work and clean off her desk. She really didn't leave very much later than the rest of the staff, only about twenty-five minutes, but it was long enough. It was more than long enough.

Kate was wary as she walked out to her car. One hand held her car keys, the ignition key between her thumb and forefinger and the rest threaded through her fingers, ready to scratch anyone who came near her. In her other hand, hidden in her pocket, she held a small can of pepper spray. It was the first time she had been alone since Jerry had vandalized her house. She knew one of John's security men was watching her, but she declined his escort to her car. Part of her whispered that if Jerry was going to come after her, let him come. She was getting impatient with being guarded and the restrictions it placed on her life.

She was also tired of the daily drills John and Bob both gave her in self-defense. John knew martial arts and Bob, she was shocked to learn, stayed in shape with a combination of weight lifting and boxing! It seemed he had two old friends, one of whom was a bodybuilder and the other a retired boxer. He worked out regularly with both of them.

Aside from the drills, Kate was armed with pepper spray and a whistle. She still knew that if Jerry wanted to get to her, he could. After all, with less than a week of instruction she was still a novice in self-defense. Also, she sensed that Jerry must be clever since he had not gotten caught. In fact, there had not been a trace of him since he'd vandalized their homes.

Kate felt it was time for her to get on with her life, even if he might make an attempt to get her. Despite her caution, just as she unlocked her car door suddenly, from out of nowhere, Jerry was there. He was standing about ten feet away, hidden in some bushes, and had a gun pointed directly at her. It was almost exactly what John and Bob had feared.

They had instructed her on how to act, and had given her a set of signals for her to let the guards know what was going on. They had both discussed ideas with her, ways to protect herself, ways to deal with Jerry, and things to watch out for. Since she knew they were being watched, and since Jerry was armed, she decided to go along with him. All of her workouts had not shown her how to disarm a man who stayed cautiously out of reach, and it was too windy for the pepper spray to be effective.

It wasn't that she was being used to bait a trap so much as the fact that all of them were aware that she *was* the bait, the focus of

Jerry's bitter anger, frustration and hatred. No one seemed to want to say it outright, but she was the target for his hatred. He blamed her for his problems: The loss of his job and his future, and the fact that there was a warrant out for his arrest. He was blaming her and denying that he was in any way to blame for his situation. She was his way of diverting the responsibility for his ruined life away from himself. They had known he would come after her. He had to try to get his revenge.

Kate tried to keep herself from looking around for the security guard she knew John had assigned to protect her, but she was too terrified to keep her eyes straight ahead. She knew she had to stall for time. If Jerry panicked or realized he was being watched, he could shoot her on the spot, and no guard alive would be able to save her.

She willed herself to relax and think but with only partial success. The one thing that scared her the most was Jerry's obvious fear and anxiety. The man was clearly coming unraveled.

"Hi Jerry." She failed miserably in her attempt to sound normal and relaxed. "How are you?"

"Shut up and get in the car, you stupid bitch, or I'll kill you right here. Not another word," Jerry said in a rough voice.

This man was a stranger who bore no resemblance to the gentle, jovial man she knew from work.

"Get in and drive where I tell you to go, and keep your stupid mouth shut."

"Why are you doing this?" she choked out. "You can't get away."

"I can and I will," he spat back at her. "I was doing fine until you stuck your nose in my business. You've ruined my life."

"You ruined your own life, Jerry. I only found the theft," she said softly, "you committed it."

In an attempt to stall for time and to avoid getting into a car with Jerry, she had been told to try to get him to talk to her. As a plan, it was logical but in practice it proved difficult given the state of near panic she was in.

No words came to mind and her throat was so tight she knew if the words did come she couldn't get them out. The reality of the situation was that Jerry refused to talk to her unless she got into the car and started driving.

It was against everything John and Bob had told her but she finally did get into the car. He sat in the passenger seat, pointing the gun at her. He turned the rearview mirror to watch for any cars following them. Then, finally, he opened up and relaxed his vigilance enough to talk to Kate.

"You ruined my life! What right did you have to go nosing around in my business? Did it make you feel powerful to cause me so much trouble?" he accused her, shouting.

"I didn't ruin your life! You did that all by yourself." She refused to take the blame for the fiasco he had made of his life. "I was brought in just for that purpose, to find a thief. I did not force you to steal and point suspicion on others. Take some responsibility, Jerry. It was you who stole money from your employer. It was you who tried to divert the blame to others. It was your crime and it's your responsibility. Only your respon- sibility. Why should I feel any sympathy for you? What about the people who were fired for something that you did? Did you enjoy ruining their lives and their futures? Did that make *you* feel powerful?"

"They were only clerks. Female clerks. They can get jobs anywhere," he grimaced, "or find a man to support them, that's what you women do best, isn't it? But I was more than a clerk, I worked hard for years and I had finally worked my way up to a management position."

Her curiosity got to her. "Jerry, how did you know that I was the one who figured it out? How did you find out I was the auditor?"

"I knew Bob was suspicious, he was sure the thefts were not being done by the accounting clerks. I knew he was getting nosy, investigating some of the others in the firm." He grinned, a sly grin. "I half expected him to bring in an auditor or an investigator when all of a sudden he hired you. I broke into his office and found several file folders that seemed out of place so I followed him a couple of nights. He always went to your house. At first, I thought it was just an office affair but then I saw him taking boxes containing those files into your house."

Kate remembered John telling her repeatedly what to do if this ever happened. Keep Jerry talking. That would do two things, hopefully: It would force Jerry to see Kate instead of a hostage; it would also lower his guard, keeping him distracted from anybody following them or setting up a trap to catch him.

"How did you do it?" she asked him, even though she knew most of the details.

"It was easy. I just duplicated some of the purchase orders, but I altered the vendor's name and address. Then I doctored the receiving slips enough to match the phony purchase orders. I sent invoices for those purchases using a post office box as a return address," he explained. "When you paid the phony invoices, the checks would go into a bank account I had set up."

"Then," he continued, "I got some false identification with Bob's name and address. Using the ID, I withdrew the money from the fake accounts and deposited it into a second account with another phony name and ID. When I needed it, I made cash withdrawals. Some of the money was in a safe deposit box in my real name, and I sent some out of the country, too."

"You went to a lot of trouble, at least two sets of fake identification and signature cards supposedly signed by Bob and Laura. Phony corporate papers for false companies, forged purchase orders, shipping receipts, and invoices. Was it worth it?" she asked. "Getting hold of some of those things must have been difficult and very expensive."

"I cleared over a hundred and fifty thousand dollars over and above my salary and the costs of getting phony documents," he bragged, "in just over a year."

"You'll never get to spend it," she told him. "Not another dime."

"All I need to do is use you as a hostage to get out of the country. I have a lot of the money in a numbered account in the Cayman Islands and a lot of cash," he snarled at her. "Besides, I already spent a lot of the money trying to keep my wife from getting beat up or killed for her gambling debts. They were even threatening to come after me."

"You must love her a lot," Kate said softly. "That was what made it so hard to track you. We couldn't find any reason for you to have such a great demand for money. You don't have large credit card debt, no kids in college, no sign of drug use, and no woman on the side. It was hard to figure out why you needed so much money. It wasn't you with a hidden vice, it was your wife. She gambles. You must love her. You risked your lifestyle and your future to save her."

"Love her, hate her," Jerry's voice trailed off, "what's the difference? She ran off and left me when she found out I was embezzling. She called me a dirty little thief."

They drove to a small, cheap motel just off the main highway. Kate pulled the car to a stop in the parking lot at the front in full view of the street, but Jerry told her to move the car around back, out of sight. He already had a room and a key. As they entered the small, tacky motel room Kate fought herself to keep from looking around for one of John's men or for a policeman. She felt a dread that surpassed all of her previous terror as she stepped into the room. Her worst fears were realized when Jerry forced her to sit on a plain wooden chair.

"Please don't tie me up, Jerry," she pleaded as she saw him pulling a length of cord out of his pocket.

"Shut up!" He slapped her and threatened, "Or I'll gag you as well."

He tied her hands together behind the back of the chair, then he tied her feet to the legs of the chair.

As he tied her hands Kate struggled and fought him hard enough to sprain her wrist, but he managed to get the knots tied. Then he did the one thing that broke her completely. She screamed as she saw him pull out a roll of duct tape that he used to cover her mouth. For a long, terrorizing moment she saw something cold mingled with the madness and hatred in his eyes, she saw the temptation to use just a little more tape, not much, just enough to cover her nostrils along with her mouth.

Kate had long since realized that Jerry was insane but now she knew, with dreadful certainty, that if she wasn't rescued he would kill her. She began to shake as tears ran down her face and she sniffled behind the mask covering her mouth.

She kept reminding herself that John had men watching her. They had been aware that sooner or later Jerry would make some kind of attack on her. They had planned to capture Jerry before he got this far with her. Why had they let him take her? The gun, she realized, they hadn't counted on him getting so close to her with a gun. There was no record of him owning a gun and embezzlement was a white-collar crime, not a violent crime. They hadn't taken his fury, his madness, his unbalanced state into account.

Kate sat there, finally going numb, terrified and cold. She thought about her kids and Bob. She tried to will herself to concentrate on everything loving and beautiful in her life. She reassured herself with the knowledge that John's men had followed them, and had already contacted the police.

She even fought the mundane battle of trying to avoid thinking about how much she wanted to go to the bathroom. That small distraction was almost a blessing, an annoying blessing.

It seemed like she was tied there for hours but it was only about thirty minutes before Jerry, who was constantly staring out the window, began to see activity outside the small motel.

"Something's up," he told her, for the first time using an almost conversational tone as he spoke to her. "The other guests are leaving their rooms."

Outside the window, that was exactly what was happening. It was like a weird migration, all the hotel guests leaving quickly and quietly, without any luggage. One or two of the guests were only partially dressed as they scurried out and got into their cars and drove out of the motel's parking lot.

"They're leaving but no one seems to be driving away. They seem to be going across the street," he said with a nervous laugh. "I've seen some of the cars pull into the shopping center and park in front of the supermarket facing the motel."

He paced around the room for a while. At one point he walked over and slapped Kate hard enough to knock her over, chair and all. She felt the scrape of the cheap carpet and smelled the faint hint of dirt and mildew in it.

While he paced, he kicked her several times as she lay on the floor catching her in the ribs and on her thighs, although she tried to roll up and prevent him from getting a good kick to her stomach.

Soon he returned to the window, cautiously standing to one side as he watched the final guests depart. The departure of the other motel guests almost diverted his attention from the legion of police officers creeping up to surround the room. Nothing could divert his attention enough to make him fail to notice the fleet of squad cars parked all over the street.

"There's enough police cars parked around the motel to catch the whole Capone mob and Bonnie and Clyde all at once," he complained.

Kate heard an unusual car horn. It was her signal to try to divert Jerry's attention. She began to make as much sound as she could in spite of the tape over her mouth. Finally, exasperated by the collection of groans and whimpers coming from behind the tape, Jerry pulled it off her mouth. Kate yelped from the pain of the ripping tape, then began to argue loudly and petulantly that she wanted to be untied because she had to go to the bathroom! It was the first diversion that came to her mind, and it had the dubious bonus of being the truth. He refused to untie her but he did lift her enough to set the chair upright again.

Her ploy failed to get Jerry far enough away from the window, and did not stop him from peaking out to watch the activity in the street. She couldn't think of another plan. She gritted her teeth and, like a scene from an old movie, began to rock the chair. It was a struggle but she managed to tip the chair back over onto its side. She gave a loud yelp as she tumbled to the floor once again, and finally got some of Jerry's attention away from the window. He came over to jerk both her and the chair upright again but she wanted to stay down. She resisted him by going limp and causing him to contend with her dead weight.

As soon as Jerry had moved away from the window the police shot teargas into the room, shattering the window. The thick cloud of caustic fumes immediately filled the room. Jerry tried to withstand the gas and fumes but dropped his weapon and collapsed to the floor.

Several officers in gas masks entered the room. Two of them quickly secured the weapon and handcuffed Jerry. The other two grabbed Kate, chair and all, and carried her from the room. Bob and John ran over to where the officers set Kate's chair down. As soon as Kate was cut loose from the chair Bob enfolded her in his arms. He kissed her tenderly, and she knew it was finally over. Bob rode with John in the car behind the ambulance as she was then transported to the nearest medical center to be treated for any effects from the tear gas, as well as checked for any other injuries from Jerry's rough treatment.

While she waited impatiently for the emergency room doctor to treat her Bob stayed by her side. She was shaking violently with delayed reaction, and there were tears streaming down her face. She knew that not all of the tears were from the teargas. She also felt nauseous. When the doctor came in, she sent Bob away while she worked on Kate.

Before leaving, Bob took the doctor aside and made a small request. Then he went to use the phone to make a few very important calls. The last call was to Ida.

As usual the doctor's first question was a blunt, "Are you pregnant?"

Kate shrugged, biting her lip and trying to count in her head, "I suppose it's possible, barely possible, but it's far too soon to tell."

"How long?" she asked in a clinical tone.

"Three weeks," Kate answered, "but it's doubtful, there was only one time that we forgot to be careful."

"And how many times does it take?" the doctor chided gently.

"With me, I get pregnant even thinking about it," Kate admitted, managing a small grin. "I have three kids already."

"I'm going to treat you as if you are pregnant but I don't see any reason to test you yet. Unless you want to know right away?" the doctor asked.

"I'm not worried about it. If I don't find out in another week or so, I'll take a home test." Kate smiled. "I told Bob that we'd have quadruplets because twins run in both our families."

"Oh, you wicked woman. Did he buy that?" the doctor asked, smiling.

"No, but he can't totally dismiss it either," Kate told her. "He shrugs it off and then gets this weird look on his face."

"Good," the doctor smiled wickedly, "keep him guessing." She got down to business. "I know he kicked you, did he manage to kick you in the abdomen?"

"Not a hard kick, I curled up the best I could," Kate told her. "He got my ribs once pretty good though."

Now that some of her good humor had been restored Kate

underwent the rest of the exam and treatment with quiet patience, although it was unnerving that Jerry had been handcuffed and brought to the same hospital. Part of her brain kept screaming, he's here!

Gradually she began to feel better aside from a few bruises, some sore ribs, and the lingering effects of the teargas. When the doctor finished with her the police asked her a few questions. She made arrangements to go to the station for a full statement the next day. Bob drove her to his house and took gentle, loving care of her.

There was a gift-wrapped box about the size of a shirt box, only quite a bit deeper, waiting on the steps to his house. It was wrapped in all-occasion paper, a colorful floral print, and had a large pink bow on it. Bob picked it up and handed it to Kate.

"I'm really excited for you to open this. In fact, I can't wait for you to open it, but I have to tell you first that I had to have a lot of help getting it put together." He kissed her, draping an arm around her shoulder. "Come inside and open it. Then I'll tell you about all the people who helped me put this together."

She went into the house with him. The gleam in his eye told her it was a very special gift, and she was so excited by it that for once she had no patience with the dogs as they greeted her. The puppies were fenced into the kitchen, but Teddy and Charger could jump the barrier and roam throughout the house.

"Go take a quick shower before you open this." He kissed her and told her firmly, "You still have traces of teargas on you. It's making me cry."

"You should feel it from my side," she quipped.

She had changed into a pair of scrubs at the hospital, but without a shower Bob was right, the gas was clinging to her. She went upstairs to take a quick shower while Bob went into the kitchen and fed the puppies. He mashed up some puppy food and puppy formula into a soggy mess, then he shut the two older dogs outside so the little guys could eat. They ate sloppily, climbing right into the shallow pan with the tiny amount of food. When they seemed finished, he used a slightly damp paper towel to clean them off. When he let the proud parents in, they licked the pan dry and then started licking and cleaning the puppies.

He poured a couple of sodas and took them into the den. Soon Kate came back downstairs. She was in an extra-long T-shirt, one that hung almost to her knees, and her hair was still damp. There was a faint bruise on one cheek, a bit of rug burn on the other, and her eyes were still red. She sat beside him on the sofa and reached for her gift. When she had the box opened and looked at the contents, she sat there speechless looking at Bob. There were tears in her eyes and she was swallowing hard.

"God, I love you. I can't think of another man who would do something like this for me." She kissed him tenderly.

"I wanted to give you back your memories." Bob hugged her. "And, I had a lot of help. Your parents, Ida and Laura were all in on this."

There were two photo albums in the box. The first one, the top one, was filled with pictures of her kids as babies. There were pictures of Joe with the kids. There were even some of Joe and her alone. The second album was almost an exact recreation of her wedding album.

"How . . ." Her voice failed.

"I've been calling everyone for at least a week nagging them to look through their old pictures for some of you and Joe, or old pictures of your kids. Your mother had quite a few, and so did Ida. We had some of the torn pictures restored by a photo studio that the Ad Company uses. Then we were really lucky when we found out where your wedding photographer had his office now. Laura knew his name but he'd moved. We called him. He had copies of all these in storage."

"Thank you." She met his eyes, her gratitude shining in hers.

"I also had the pictures put on a photo disc and had the disc copied so that one set could be put in a safety deposit box. That way they can never be lost again." He smiled at her. "Now, can I see them? I can't wait to look at them with you."

They sat side by side on the sofa. Kate showed him the pictures and somehow along the way, introduced him to Joe. Bob got a feeling for the kind of man he was: handsome, loving and laughing, but also a bit gruff. They looked at her wedding pictures. It had been a large formal wedding with all the trimmings.

"Would you want another fancy wedding like that if you ever got married again?" Bob asked her, trying to sound casual.

"I don't think so. It was beautiful, but it was frankly a pain in the behind to pull it all together." She cuddled up to him. "By the time my wedding day finally arrived, I was too tired to really enjoy it. The important the thing is having the people you love around you and marrying the right person. The ceremony is sacred of course, but the wedding stuff itself is all flash and fancy trappings. Who cares about the flowers, limos, and reception food, not to mention little details like napkins imprinted with your names and fancy place settings? Ugh! We even had matchbooks with our names on them and neither one of us smoked! The marriage is the important part, and that comes after the ceremony and the party ends."

"That makes sense," Bob agreed. "I never realized weddings were so much work."

"You should read one of those books on how to plan a wedding." She shivered. "They have pages and pages of lists and little calendars that tell you how long before the wedding you should have each item on each list completed."

In response Bob gave a low whistle and said, "Sounds like a mess."

"So," she gave him a saucy grin, "why are you so interested in my opinion of weddings?"

"No special reason, just making conversation, my love." He kissed her. "Let's get the puppies, I want to play."

"You used to like to play with me." Her lower lip stuck out.

"We can do that too, if you want," Bob kissed her, "but I thought you might still be feeling a little queasy."

"You're right, bring on the little guys." She smiled.

"Hey, by the way, I called your mom. She's bringing the kids home tomorrow," Bob told her casually, turning back to see her pleased expression.

He brought the puppies in, along with Teddy and Charger. Kate and Bob got down on the floor and played with the little family until the puppies were tired. Then they put the litter back in the kitchen and made themselves a light dinner of soup and sandwiches. Finally, hand in hand, they went up to bed.

Chapter Fourteen

The week following Jerry's capture turned out to be very busy and happy for both Kate and Bob. Kate's mother and grandmother flew home with the kids as soon as Bob called them, arriving early the next day. It seemed strange for Kate to realize that Bob had not met her mother. Introductions took second place, however, to the excitement of her kids when they saw the puppies. All the adults were kept busy rescuing the little black and white bundles of love from overzealous little fingers. Watching them, Kate knew she was right to keep the kids away from the puppies for a couple of weeks. If the kids had been just a bit older, she would have handled it differently, but this time it seemed the right thing to do.

Kate's mother and grandmother seemed to take to Bob really well. They remarked on his manners and his patience with the kids. They asked him about his family, his job, and his plans for the future.

Kate's grandmother took Kate aside. "Katie girl, that man is as nice as he can be, and he loves you. I want you to think about one thing though: Do you want to wind up with a man like that?"

"Yes, Grandma. I want him. What's wrong with him?" Kate asked, disappointed that her grandma seemed to have reservations about Bob.

"Nothing at all is wrong with him, Dearie. Not one damn thing." Her grandma winked and continued, "I just thought if you didn't want him, I'd make a play for him myself. That man is *tasty*."

"Granny!" Kate almost choked laughing.

"Hey!" She hugged Kate and said, "I'm old, not senile."

185

While Kate and Bob were at work each day, Kate's mother and grandma helped her finish up the last minute details of redecorating Bob's house and getting it ready for the family reunion which was set for the following weekend. There was almost no time to plan everything, but Bob's family was eager to meet Kate. Kate's mom and grandma did massive amounts of shopping, both for home decor and for food, and they spent hours cooking. Kate's father spent a lot of time at Bob's that week; he had to, it was where his wife, his daughter and the food were.

Kate was a hero when she returned to work that week. The office girls were very concerned and upset about her kidnapping. So concerned that it was overwhelming. By midday Tuesday she was already tired of the constant pampering and attention. She just wanted to dig into her workload. Her paperwork was piled sky high on her desk and she had two women to interview for the Accounts Payable position.

Then to top it off, the company president flew in from corporate headquarters in Texas for an unexpected business. The rumor around the office was that his visit involved the company thefts and also company policies regarding romance between fellow employees.

The president ensconced himself in Bob's office with Bob. It seemed like hours before anyone went in or came out. Kate tried to concentrate on her work but it was extremely difficult to avoid staring at the office door and wondering what was being said in that office.

The president finally came over to Kate's small cubicle and introduced himself. He was a gruff man, mid-fifties, portly and handsome, dressed in a formal charcoal gray business suit. He looked over everything Kate had done. He questioned her about working at home investigating the thefts, and the backlog in Accounts Payable. With an unsmiling face, he asked her bluntly about her relationship with Bob, how it started and whether she felt it affected her job performance. After she answered his questions, he abruptly stood and left her cubicle. Kate shivered as she watched him walk back to Bob's office. Once inside Bob's office, he sat on the plush sofa without saying a word.

Finally he said, "Damn it Bob, I know you have some bourbon in here. I put in the bar myself. Pour me a drink!" Bob poured him bourbon from the bottle he kept just for him.

When it was in his hand, he drank some and sighed, "You know what the company policy is on dating between employees."

"Yes, I do." Bob was reserved and cautious.

"God knows what the policy is on marriage between employees. I don't." He sipped his drink. "What a mess! I don't want to lose you; you're damn good at this job and well liked by the staff. I also don't want to lose her, she has a lot on the ball and I wasn't easy on her out there. Looks good, too."

"So?" Bob asked.

"So, if you two marry, I can guarantee that your jobs will not be threatened in any way." He smiled, "You'd be a damn fool to pass up a woman like that, and who wants a damn fool working for them? I certainly don't!"

"Can you stay for the weekend?" Bob asked, feeling like a weight was lifted from his shoulders. "We're having a party and I have a surprise for everyone, including Kate."

"I can't, my wife's birthday is coming and if I miss it, I'm a dead man." He sipped again. "So what's your surprise? I won't tell."

Bob told him everything. The president laughed and said, "Maybe I'll fly the wife out here, I've got to see this!" He sobered and asked in wonder, "But what'll you do if she says no?"

Bob had a very busy week ahead of him, but no one else knew it. He spent almost every second on the phone, to the point of making Kate feel almost neglected. He also spent massive amounts of money trying to get everything done in record time.

Except for his mother, even his own family wasn't aware of his plan.

Her response when she heard was a concerned, "What'll you do if she says no?"

Kate, unaware of Bob's plotting, barely had time to feel neglected since she was also very busy. She had hired a professional cleaning crew to come in and finish cleaning out her house, shampoo her carpets and clean her windows and drapes. Then she had some very basic furniture delivered, beds and mattresses, a kitchen table, a sofa and television, just enough to make the house livable. Kate and Bob would stay in the house from Thursday night throughout the reunion, leaving his house for his parents and his brother and his family.

Bob's family began to gather for the reunion the following Thursday. His parent's flight in from Reno landed Thursday afternoon, and Kate and Bob had dinner with them that evening. Bob's parents were warm, friendly people. His brother, Jeff, and his family arrived Friday evening. There was a spaghetti dinner with Bob, Kate, her kids, Bob's parents, his brother and his family Friday night. To Kate's surprise, Bob had also invited Ida. Together with George, they were both made to feel like part of the family.

By Saturday morning Bob's house was a zoo, filled with Bob's family. Kate's parents, along with Bob and Kate were there much of the time, and of course, the dogs and puppies, too. Bob's sisters and both their families drove in. One sister lived to the south, near San Diego. The other sister and her family lived to the north, near San Bernardino. They were just far enough apart to make it a special occasion for everyone to get together.

Once the group had assembled and Kate's kids were included, there were thirteen kids, all under eleven.

All the parents involved had a nightmare trying to keep both kids and dogs out of the swimming pool, even though there was an adult appointed to act as lifeguard at all times and a separate locked fence was around the pool. For the barbecue on Saturday night, friends and co-workers and their families had been invited, too. The barbecue was started late in the afternoon, and it was in use for the rest of the day; plus there were salads, breads, pies, cakes and homemade ice cream, all kinds of delicious food.

They had a stereo system set up on the patio, so Bob invited his neighbors. He was copying Laura's idea, attempting to keep them from complaining about the noise. With Bob's neighbors it worked like a charm. As long as there was food and fun and they were invited to join in, they were willing to put up with the noise. He even invited Kate's neighbor, Tim, but she wasn't too disappointed when he declined. She was shocked that the corporate president showed up with his wife, even more so that he was cordial and charming. In fact, the man seemed outright happy. She was speechless when she later found out that he'd flown his wife in just for the event.

The most common topic of conversation, after horror tales about Kate's short-lived kidnapping, was marriage. Specifically, when were Kate and Bob getting married? Every time he was asked about it, Bob told the person to ask him again, later. Or ask him tomorrow. Kate's answer was simpler. "He hasn't asked me, and I haven't asked him."

Before the night was over, Ida asked her when the wedding would be. She told Kate she had her blessing as long as she was still considered part of the family.

Kate hugged her and said simply, "You will always be part of my family. You gave me Joe."

Later even her kids had asked if she was going to marry Bob. She talked to them, trying to reassure herself that they liked Bob, and would be happy to have him as a new daddy. She also wanted to avoid getting their hopes up because there wasn't an engagement, yet.

Saturday night, after everyone but family had gone home,

Kate and Bob went back to her house. Bob's brother and his family were staying in his house. With the few pieces of furniture Kate had bought, they had fixed things up at her house just enough to make it nice and comfortable for the night. Although Kate was still excited to have her kids home, they left them at Bob's house to play with his brother's kids. The privacy was wasted though in terms of lovemaking because between their heavy workloads, arranging the parties, following up with the insurance companies and police, and Kate's bruised ribs, they only slept that night.

Sunday was another beautiful late summer day. Everyone could tell Bob had something special set up. There was something about him, both tense and excited at once. Somehow, even though it was a last minute affair he had managed to rent the banquet hall at a nearby hotel, complete with a catered meal, and invited everyone, family, friends and even co-workers.

He had also rented an extra suite near the banquet room and hired two members of the hotel staff to act as babysitters. In that suite they had games and toys for all the kids, plus videos and some special refreshments. There was also a place for tired kids to go and rest; and after a hefty bribe paid to the hotel manager, even a place for the dogs and puppies.

The banquet room was filled to overflowing with flowers, all in shades of pink, yellow and peach. The setting was beautiful and the appetizers were fantastic. But the prime rib dinner was delayed. No one really minded since there was an open bar and a good live band. The whole party was extravagant, but all the guests, friends and family alike were puzzled.

Weren't family reunions supposed to be noisy affairs held outdoors? Picnics and barbecues, with games and laughter? Bob kept insisting it was perfectly normal to have a fancy dinner for friends and family. He said over and over that he just wanted everyone to have a wonderful time, to be totally comfortable and relaxed. He explained that he didn't want the women to have to spend the day cooking or looking after kids.

Besides, he went on, seeming just a little nervous, this party gave everyone a chance to get dressed up. The new family pictures would be beautiful. Most of the friends and family just drank the champagne and kept their thoughts to themselves but the word was out, this had all the earmarks of an engagement party. A surprise engagement party.

Kate made her way around the room greeting everyone. She stopped to speak with Lanie. Although they barely knew each other, she had made a special effort to get Lanie to attend. Partly, of course, because of her matchmaking efforts with Frank.

"I'm so glad you came," Kate greeted the woman. "Please have some champagne and here's some cider for your daughter." She handed them matching champagne flutes. She spoke with Lanie's daughter, Cassie and told her about the kids' room. She offered to take Cassie there herself and suggested that Lanie go over and talk to Frank.

When she returned from the kids' room, she walked over to the bar for some champagne and found a quiet seat to relax for a second. Seeing her sitting there, Laura came over to Kate; for once she was subtle as she tried to pump her friend for the inside story.

"You look beautiful, Kate." She hugged her best friend. "Is that a new dress?"

Kate looked down at what was indeed a new dress; a soft tangerine-colored cocktail dress cut with a rounded scooped neck. It was highlighted with subtle beading on the bodice, and the skirt was full and swirled as she walked. She had set her hair then left it loose and free, curling almost down to her waist.

"Thanks, Laura. Bob bought it for me." Kate smiled at the thought. "Let's walk over to that open doorway, it's hot in here."

The two women strolled over to the open French doors. There was a lull in the conversation until finally Laura asked Kate outright, "Is this an engagement party or what?"

"Beats me." Kate shrugged.

"I do not!" Bob came up behind her, sliding his arms around her waist.

"I was just trying to find out when you two are getting married," Laura asked him.

Bob got a laughable look on his face and turned to Laura. "Give us a few minutes alone, okay Laura?"

Then he turned to face Kate and waited a minute to let Laura walk away. Laura went, but not very far. This sounded promising! She strained her ears, trying to listen.

Ida saw her interest and came over to join her. "Is he finally proposing?"

"I think so." Laura took the older woman's hand. "Isn't it romantic?"

Ida laughed, "Only if she says yes, my dear. Only if she says yes."

Bob looked at Kate, wondering how he could keep his knees from knocking. She looked back at him in an agony of suspense. Ask me, she willed silently, ask me. Her heart was beating so hard she thought everyone could hear it, but she looked at him silently, finally raising one eyebrow and tilting her head.

Bob took a deep breath. "Kate, will you marry me?"

"Yes." Kate laughed and threw her arms around his neck. "Oh yes. Even though that was the least romantic, skimpiest proposal I ever heard. No loving declarations, no down on one knee. Just five short words."

"Do you want all the fancy stuff?" Bob looked around the room. "I can get down on one knee if you want."

"No, love. You give me all the romance I could handle everyday." She hugged him. "Besides, I accepted the proposal you gave me. I had already heard all the other pretty words from you; those five were the exact ones I was waiting for."

As they kissed, Laura and Ida came over. "So is it finally official?"

"Yes," Kate smiled at her friend, her face glowing, "we're going to be married."

The two women watched as Bob produced a small jeweler's box that held an engagement ring and slid it onto her finger. It was an emerald cut diamond with baguettes that fit perfectly.

"The ring's gorgeous! When?" Laura questioned. "When is the wedding? God! There's so much planning to do!"

"I don't know, yet." Kate turned to Bob and asked, "When do you think we should get married?"

"I'd like to get married right now." For the second time that day Bob had a strange look on his face.

"So would I, but we need blood tests and a license, all that stuff." Kate dismissed the idea. "And a minister or somebody who could perform the ceremony."

"Actually, I meant it," Bob said, looking a little flushed. "You may not realize this but we had our blood tests when you were in the hospital, and I pulled a few strings so we also have a license. It was so easy to get your signature on the form; you'll sign anything I put in front of you." He smiled and then paused, catching his breath. "Everybody we know and love is here, and your kids are dressed up. They've even managed to stay clean." He nervously pointed out a man across the room. "And that's Fred Dawson, the minister from my church."

"You mean it?" Kate was stunned and excited. "Now?"

"Just pick out your Maid of Honor, and I'll ask my brother to be my Best Man." Bob looked at her, a look that filled her heart. "I even have a rack with several wedding dresses stashed nearby in case you wanted to wear a more traditional gown. As long as you don't feel rushed or forced into anything."

"No, you've just saved me the trouble of dragging you to the altar. Plus you saved me all the bother that goes into planning a wedding." She grinned. "So what's the hold up? Let's do it."

"Laura, do me a favor," Bob asked her. "Go get my brother and Fred. Oh, and ask the waiter by the door to tell the banquet manager the wedding's on. He's got the flowers and cake."

Laura agreed excitedly to run the errands. As she turned to walk away a thought struck her, "Bob, what if she'd said no?"

"That's easy," Bob grinned, "I'd have sicced you on her."

After Laura left Kate looked up at Bob, a question in her happy eyes. "How did you manage to do all this?"

"It was easy, I got hold of one of those books on wedding planning, hired a team of wedding planners, and enlisted all the help I could without giving myself away," he bragged with a cheeky grin.

Soon, Bob and Kate were standing on the dais at the front of the room. There was a microphone and Bob spoke into it.

"Excuse me, everybody. May I have your attention?" He waited for the guests to settle down and look up at him. "I have two things to tell you. The first one probably won't surprise any of you. Kate has accepted my proposal of marriage." He paused for a long moment to let the group react. "Wait! There's more." He held up his hand to stop the guests from rushing up to the stage to congratulate them.

"Don't tell me, let me guess." Kate's mother had made it to the dais and hugged her daughter and Bob. "Didn't anyone ever tell you it was tacky to announce your wedding and your pregnancy at the same time?" she asked in a low voice.

Bob's face got red and he looked at Kate with a question in his eyes. She shrugged, grinned sheepishly, and made a gesture with her hands that seemed to say, "Who knows?"

"No Mom, that's not it." Kate grinned. "At least it would be news to me."

"So what's the second announcement?" she asked her daughter with exasperation and maybe just a touch of disappointment in her voice.

Bob went back to the microphone. "The second announcement may surprise you. It surprised Kate." He grinned at Kate who gave him a companionable but slightly off-kilter grin in return. "The second announcement is that the wedding is right here and now. Jeff, I need you to act as my Best Man."

There was a surprised murmur from the guests. The hotel staff got busy opening a partition and expanding the banquet room, revealing that it had another dais surrounded by flowers. There was an aisle with a long white carpet runner down the middle of the chairs. The seats lining the aisle had a long garland of white ribbons and pale roses that matched Kate's dress stretching from the first row to the last.

Kate stared in amazement as she saw the banquet staff wheel a small table over near the buffet. It contained a four-tiered wedding cake with forks, plates and a champagne fountain. While the last few details were being seen to, Bob and Kate walked around the room accepting hugs and congratulation from friends and family. She sipped a glass of champagne, feeling dazed.

Her mother and father volunteered to keep the kids for that night, but it was decided that the kids would stay with Bob's brother. Bob had booked a suite in the hotel for their honeymoon night. Then he announced they would both take a full week off work leaving Laura slightly overwhelmed with all the responsibility, and take the kids to the local amusement parks: Disneyland and Knott's Berry Farm. Laughing, he invited his brother and his wife to stay over a few days to join them at Disneyland.

"It may be a little unconventional, but so is this whole wedding. Besides, your kids should get to see Mickey while they're in California." Bob grinned.

Laughing, his brother agreed.

Later, on her way around the room, Kate was surprised to see the doctor who had treated her at the emergency room after her kidnapping.

The doctor hugged her and took her aside. She explained to Kate, "I told Bob that my price for sneaking that blood test through was an invitation to the wedding." She continued, "I thought a surprise wedding sounded so romantic."

"I never did get around to making an appointment for that other test, and I definitely should take it," Kate told her.

"I knew it. Well, call me when you have time, unless you already have a regular doctor." She told Kate where her practice was.

"I will. To tell you the truth, I think it's a strong probability. I guess Bob isn't the only one who can spring surprises on people." Kate was floating, still feeling surprised and shocked. "I may have to go to some extreme lengths to top his though."

She made her way over to her father. "Happy for me, Daddy?"

"Beyond words, sweetie. He's a wonderful man. He'll make you very happy." Her father kissed her gently on the forehead.

The office staff came over as a group to congratulate both of them; Kate was swept up in a storm of loving tears and hugs. Leaving that group she went over to where Bob's parents and his sisters were standing.

"I hope you're all happy. This is a complete surprise to me, but I couldn't be happier." She hugged Bob's mother.

"I knew I would get a new daughter someday, but I never dreamed she'd be so special." She kissed Kate on the cheek. "And I get three more grandchildren, adorable grandchildren, as a bonus."

All of Kate's new family made her feel loved and welcomed. Kate wouldn't have believed she could get any happier, but she could. She found Bob and linked her arm in his, still accepting heartfelt congratulations and love from her friends.

There was a broad smile on her face as she considered the very real possibility of becoming a mother again sooner than anyone expected, but she kept that thought to herself. She would share it with Bob later, in private. On her wedding night, she thought to herself, feeling giddy.

Laura came over to her and together they went to the room

where Bob had arranged for a selection of bridal gowns to be waiting. She found one that fit her perfectly. It had a square neckline with a beaded bodice and a softly flowing, floor-length skirt of silky satin.

Finally everything was arranged for the wedding and the hotel staff turned their attention to organizing the first banquet room for a wedding reception. They had napkins imprinted with the couple's names. There were small picture frames with the couple's names and a menu at every setting. The head table was set up for the bride and groom.

Seeing some of this, Jack asked Bob, "Hey old buddy, how did you know about all this stuff?"

"I bought a wedding planning book." He seemed slightly embarrassed as he admitted it. "Plus I remembered one of my sisters going on and on about something on Oprah, about some of the fanciest wedding of the year. When I called her she said there was a story about the wedding in Women's Day magazine and faxed me some of it."

Seemingly, from out of nowhere, a photographer and a videographer appeared. The minister, Fred, and Bob's brother, Jeff, made their way up to the dais. The banquet manager handed Kate a bridal bouquet and pinned a matching corsage on Laura. He pinned boutonnieres on Bob and Jeff.

Then Bob, adding a touch of extra love and humor to the wedding, handed both the Best Man and Matron of Honor a leash. Charger, standing by the best man had a white tuxedo collar and a black tie, and Teddy, standing by Laura had roses fastened to her collar.

Kate's kids all got flowers, too. Sam, in a miniature tux with a boutonniere, was drafted to act a ring bearer, and Suzy and Sarah were in lacy peach dresses with matching ribbons in their hair, had tiny corsages as they acted as the flower girls.

The kids made their way up the aisle, Sam solemnly carrying the rings. Sarah and Suzy got a little mixed up with the rose petals, however. The little angels threw them directly at the guests. They were a little surprised at the reaction that got as all the guests started laughing. From the back of the room Kate, filled with amusement and pride, looked at the little girls, then met Bob's eyes and saw the same proud expression shining in his eyes.

When the girls were seated by Kate's mother and grandmother, and Sam was standing next to Jeff, Laura started down the aisle. When Laura was in position at the front of the room, Kate took a deep breath. She slipped her hand into her father's arm, looked up at him with a nervous, eager little smile and began to walk down the aisle. Once at the front of the room, her father kissed her on the cheek. The minister opened his book.

"Dearly beloved," the Minister intoned, "I see we have the whole family here, including the four-legged members of the family, and friends. We have gathered together . . ."

And so the simple, loving, beautiful ceremony joining their lives together began.

Other books by Susan Kohler

The Paddle Club

Hot Crossed Buns

Another Batch of Warm Buns

The Heart of The Beast

Coming soon...

Read about Kate and Laura as they play matchmaker for Frank in:

Who's Taming Who?